To my beautiful children, Annabelle and Harry.
My very own "DNA Detectives".

Foreword

When I was at school I always loved science and I was interested in the biology of diseases. I decided to go to university so I could find out more. It was when I was there that something very magical happened; a lightbulb moment which mapped out my future career.

I was working in the laboratory on my final-year project. We were using DNA to try and identify what made mosquitoes resistant to pesticides to help reduce the number of cases of malaria. The first step in the process was to get DNA from the mosquitoes. I was on the very last stage which, in my opinion, is the most exciting. I had a tube of clear liquid which appeared to have nothing in it. Then, by adding alcohol, as if by magic, strands of DNA appeared. What was truly amazing is that the mosquito DNA was purple. I remember looking at that tube and realising the huge potential for working with DNA.

The procedures for working with DNA are the same whether you are working on plants, bacteria, humans or any other animal. So, if you have a favourite animal, the chances are that there is someone somewhere in the world using DNA to study that animal. DNA is used in so many different fields, by conservationists and naturalists to learn about different animals and plants, by forensic scientists to help solve crimes, by archaeologists to find out about the past, by clinical scientists to study inherited diseases and by scientists to identify how people are related – and that is to name but a few!

I realised in that moment when I saw the mosquito DNA in the laboratory that, if I chose to work in this particular field, I could go anywhere in the world and work on any animal or plant I wanted. There were so many different types of job available to me that, if I got bored doing one thing, I could easily transfer to something else! It really was a life-changing moment that has led to the most amazing and wonderful career. All thanks to DNA.

I have used DNA to try and help conserve stocks of haddock and sand eels in the North Sea. I have worked for the NHS using DNA to help people with breast cancer, neonatal diabetes, cystic fibrosis, haemophilia and kidney diseases. I helped set up the forensic laboratories now used by the Norfolk Constabulary and helped identify relationships for long-lost families. Now my great passion is teaching children about DNA.

I love watching children discover DNA for the first time. Much like I did in the laboratory at university. I never get tired of seeing DNA appear in a tube. Now watching children's faces light up when they see that they have successfully extracted DNA from a piece of fruit is incredibly rewarding. For many children attending my workshops this is hopefully the moment they too decide to become scientists! My feeling is that children are never too young to learn about DNA.

I hope you enjoy reading this book, finding out about DNA and how the characters in the story use DNA to solve a crime. I hope it inspires you with a love of science just like me those many years ago when I was in the laboratory and saw DNA for the first time!

**www.thelittlestorytellingcompany.co.uk/
the-dna-detectives-to-catch-a-thief**

Chapter 1

A laboratory in the garden

(F) rom the outside, Chapel Terrace was a very normal-looking street. In fact, some might have said, a very dull-looking street. (And up until recent events, they might have been right). A row of identical terraced houses faced yet another row of identical looking houses, all with a porch, cellar and a large garden to the rear. All with absolutely nothing to set them apart; except for one house, belonging to the Wallace family.

Their garden had all the usual features; grass, swings, trees, but at the back of it was something very unusual. A laboratory. And this laboratory would become the starting place for a series of unexpected adventures.

The lab belonged to Dr Wallace, Mum of Annabelle and Harry. "My mum is a scientist, who works with DNA," Annabelle would proudly tell her friends. Her mum was so smart, and so passionate, that she loved to listen to her and learn.

"DNA is a very small particle, invisible to the naked eye. It contains the entire instructions to make a human being," her mum would tell her, and Annabelle would nod, though she didn't always fully understand.

One morning, Annabelle watched as her mother started up the computer to book in the latest DNA samples that had arrived. Her eyes were drawn to the main news piece on the homepage:

"ONE MORE MISSING DOG ON CHAPEL TERRACE," read the headline on the local news site.

"Mum, Mum, look! Another dog's gone missing!" Annabelle yelled.

"What? Oh, yes, that's awful," said her mum.

"What do you think is happening to them?" Annabelle asked, glancing in fright at her own beautiful dog, Milly, as she bounded past the window towards Harry.

"I imagine they strayed too far from home, and got lost. Hopefully they'll find them soon."

"Three dogs, in three weeks? Really?" asked Annabelle, suspiciously. "Dogs are smarter than that." She took a breath, and declared, "I think someone's taking them."

Her mum laughed. Clearly she wasn't going to take Annabelle seriously on the matter, so Annabelle went outside to join Harry and Milly, chasing a model plane.

Milly – a cockapoo – was a small black dog with curly fur, a very waggy tail and brown eyes that permanently said: "I'm hungry, feed me. If you don't I shall consider you cruel and I'll starve." She considered Annabelle and Harry her puppies and took great care looking after them. Annabelle remembered the day they first brought her home. Milly kept licking her and Harry. She had felt a little unsure of the little black ball of curls until Mum had explained "puppies lick you to show affection. I think she must really like you both." Then, when they had turned round, Harry had started licking Milly all over. "No Harry!" they had shouted together and then proceeded to laugh till their sides hurt!

Sometimes, Annabelle felt a little sad when Harry and Milly played together. She wasn't as fast or as energetic as Harry, and she soon became out of breath. Sometimes when they went to the park, Harry would run off without her and Milly would follow, just to make sure he was safe. But then Annabelle would be left on her own.

Harry ran to the edge of the garden to jump at the model plane and Milly rounded him up, like a sheep dog.

"See, she loves me more than you, Annabelle," said Harry, his cheeks flushing with pride and sweat.

"It's not a competition, Harry. If I ran off she'd get me too," Annabelle defended herself, feeling protective of her own bond with Milly. Almost as if in answer, Milly bounded back and nuzzled her leg.

"Come on, children," called Mum from inside. "Or you'll be late for school! Goodness, I got so carried away with these samples."

"Please can we play with Milly just a little bit longer?" Harry pleaded, but Milly ran toward Mum, who stood tapping her watch.

✳ ✳ ✳

Later that day, in the car on the way back from school, their arguments continued.

"I clearly care about Milly more, Harry, because I always take her for a walk. If you cared you wouldn't make such a fuss."

"It doesn't matter," replied Harry, flatly.

"If she could hear you it would make her sad," announced Annabelle.

"I don't make Milly sad!" yelled Harry, outraged. "When I'm sad she always licks my tears. She obviously loves me more, even if I don't take her for a stupid walk."

"That's enough!" said Mum sternly, just as Annabelle had opened her mouth to reply. She poked her tongue out at Harry instead.

When they arrived home, Mum ushered the children out into the garden.

"Why don't you both go outside and play?" she said, glancing at the stack of samples in the corner. Annabelle knew Mum only wanted five minutes of peace to get on with her work, and so, though it was a cold, March afternoon and she would really rather be inside reading her latest book, she followed Harry into the garden.

Harry, unaware of Mum's need for quiet time, needed no persuasion to play outside at any time of year. Annabelle sat on the patio, pulling her woollen hat over her ears and watching Harry as he bounced a ball on his knee. He had crumbs on his cheek. There was always something on his face, or his clothes; a reminder of what he had done that day. Some mud from a puddle he had splashed in or some jam from the toast he had eaten earlier.

Annabelle wondered at his inexhaustible supplies of energy, and his powerful sense of adventure. He never seemed to get cold or tired. Had she been like that at eight years old? Annabelle thought not. Most of the time, Harry drove her mad. But she also admired his enthusiasm for everything, and how he could say things without overthinking them. Annabelle always thought before she spoke. Harry always made everybody laugh, and he made everything fun on his own. Annabelle needed Harry to make things feel fun.

Harry watched his sister, as she sat on the step, and wondered what she was thinking. She was tall for an eleven year old with beautiful brown curly hair, pale skin and blue eyes, like Mum. She was clever, too, thought Harry. She would always go to the science workshops with Mum, and understood things quickly. Sometimes Harry joined in, but after a few minutes went outside to play again. Not because he wasn't interested, but because he found it easier to kick a ball than to learn. Annabelle was much smarter than him, and he felt like he was asking too many questions and slowing them down. Annabelle would be a scientist like Mum, but he wouldn't, Harry thought with a sigh.

He kicked the ball towards her, and she smiled. He came forward and playfully boxed Annabelle, to which she squealed. Delighted at her response, he decided to impress her. He ran to grab his model plane, so that he would have the first throw. His blond curls bounced as he climbed as dangerously high as he could on the climbing frame to launch the plane down at Annabelle.

"Catch it!" shouted Harry.

The little plane, painted to look like a World War II Spitfire, set off at great speed as Harry launched it. Milly heard the word "catch" and decided to grab the plane in her mouth before Annabelle had the chance. She went haring round the garden, and Harry climbed down to chase her.

"This is your fault, Harry! You threw it too low!"

"What? You should've caught it!"

The little black dog weaved between the children, her tail wagging so fast it looked like it might come off. Finally she got bored and dropped it.

"You threw it too low! I'll fly it this time," said Annabelle.

She snatched it and threw it into the air. The children watched as the little plane flew high into the sky, up, up and over the fence into the next-door neighbour's garden.

"You did that on purpose!" said Harry, bursting into tears.

"I'm really sorry, Harry," said Annabelle, feeling a rush of guilt. She knew it was his favourite plane. Just for once she had wanted to be fun and spontaneous, like Harry.

Just then there was a loud, clattering noise. A smiling face popped up from behind the fence, and peered over the top at Annabelle and Harry. It was their neighbour, Mr Baker, and he had the plane in his hand.

"Hello children, have you lost something?" he said, passing it over.

"Thank you," said Annabelle quietly, as Milly growled.

"Not at all!" answered Mr Baker, running a hand over his dark, slicked back hair. His smile stretched from ear to ear.

Milly growled. The fur on her back stood up and her ears flattened.

"Quiet Milly!" whispered Annabelle.

"Quiet Milly!" parroted Harry.

"Sorry, Mr Baker," said Annabelle, puzzled. "She's usually very friendly."

"Oh bless her," said Mr Baker. "Maybe I scared her when I popped up like that. Or maybe she just wants her plane back! She's gorgeous. How old is she?"

Harry was delighted to talk about Milly.

"She's three. She loves eating tomatoes which she steals from the vegetable rack," he said proudly.

Then Mum came out to fetch them for dinner as Dad was home. She saw Mr Baker standing by the fence. Annabelle and Harry explained what had happened, and she urged them to thank their neighbour.

"I already did! I've got manners," said Annabelle, glancing at Harry.

It was getting dark as the family sat down to eat. Sausages, beans and chips – everyone's favourite, including Milly! But, strangely uninterested in her food, Milly scratched at the back door to be let out.

"What's wrong with her today?" asked Harry.

"She growled at Mr Baker, too!" added Annabelle. "She was probably surprised when he popped up over the fence," said Dad, getting up to let her out. "And you know what she's like. She's convinced it's her job to defend the house."

They carried on eating as Milly barked outside. When they had finished their chocolate pudding and ice cream, Mum opened the back door and called Milly. Harry and Annabelle sat expectantly, waiting for their little dog to come bounding in, eager for leftovers from Annabelle to be slipped to her under the table. But she didn't come.

Dad frowned, and got up to join his wife. They went outside, calling Milly's name. Annabelle and Harry could hear their parents' shouts, but no barking in return. They looked at each other, with a sense of unspoken panic. Eventually, they put on their shoes and coats and went outside, and found Mum and Dad standing looking at the garden gate. It was swinging open.

Back inside, they frantically grabbed their torches and ran together in different directions around the village, desperately shouting Milly's name. Annabelle went with Dad, and Harry with Mum. At one point, Harry thought he saw Milly in the darkness.

"Look! Mum!" he exclaimed.

But it was just a big, black cat.

After an hour, they realised their search was in vain. When they finally returned to the house Harry, Annabelle and Mum were fighting back tears. Dad was just crying.

Milly was gone.

"Now do you believe me?" raged Annabelle.

Mum said nothing.

"Believe what?" sobbed Harry.

"There's a pet thief on Chapel Terrace," said Annabelle.

"And they've taken Milly."

Chapter 2

To catch a thief

The next morning it was cold outside but the sun shone brightly into the kitchen at Chapel Terrace. Maybe the sun was trying to lift the very grey and sad mood that gripped the house. Breakfast in the Wallace household was unusually quiet, until Annabelle broke the silence.

"I couldn't sleep last night," said Annabelle. She looked very pale and tired. The worry showed on her small face. "I kept thinking about Milly and that she was all alone. I think she'll be missing us."

"Me too," whispered Harry softly. As he said it he looked out into the garden, his head full of thoughts of Milly. "I think she'll be missing me most of all."

Annabelle would usually have argued back. She would have told Harry in no uncertain terms that Milly would not be missing him the most. She stopped herself, looking at her brother's face and catching his beautiful green eyes, normally so sparkly with fun. This morning they looked so sad. They were red and puffy just like hers. She knew exactly how he was feeling and, for once, she wanted to protect him.

"I really miss her, Mum," he said, pushing away his cereal bowl full of Coco Pops. On a normal morning he would be tipping the bowl into his mouth when Mum wasn't looking to drink the last scraps of milk. Today it had hardly been touched.

Annabelle watched Mum, watching them both. She could see that she was concerned.

"You poor things," she comforted. "Look, I'm sure Milly will turn up. In the mean time I've put a message on a lost dogs page on the internet. All the local dog owners read it. If anyone sees her I'm sure they will get in touch."

Annabelle knew that what her mum had said should reassure her. There was a chance that Milly had simply run out of the gate and got lost. But there was also the horrible possibility that Milly was the latest victim of the pet thief.

"Come on Annabelle, let's go outside," said Harry. He didn't like the doom and gloom that was filling the kitchen. It made him feel trapped like he couldn't breathe. He didn't want to tell anyone that he had cried into his pillow last night. He was trying to show everyone how brave he was. Maybe beating Annabelle at a game of football outside was what he needed. "Come on, let's play football."

Annabelle shrugged but followed him into the garden.

The grass was still wet with dew. It was one of those bright, sunny mornings when you can smell that spring is in the air. The daffodils were starting to flower and the birds tweeted away as the children went out to play. Harry, being his usual lazy self, waited for Annabelle to retrieve the ball from the flower bed for him. But as she went to pick the ball up she gasped.

"Harry! Come quickly." Harry, startled by the urgency in her voice, ran over. They both stared at the large footprint deeply embedded into the soil by the fence. Next to it was the end of a cigarette. Just above the footprint on the fence was a clump of black, curly hair and, more worryingly, a red stain that looked like blood.

"D... d... do you think it might be Milly's blood?" stammered Harry.

Thinking the worst, but wanting to reassure her frightened little brother, Annabelle said, "No. I think it's more likely that if someone did come into our garden to take Milly they could've cut themselves on the fence." Annabelle stood up straight and looked around her.

"There may other clues," she said. "Let's search the garden."

Harry ran off and shortly shouted over to Annabelle. "Look! A hat and a glove! Right here, Annabelle. They were just lying on the grass by the playhouse."

Annabelle ran over and could see there was a navy blue baseball cap lying upside down on the damp grass and a large brown leather glove. The glove had scratches all over it which you could see were deeply embedded into the surface of the leather. The glove was also heavily stained. Annabelle thought it was most likely to be the water from the wet grass that had caused it to be discoloured.

"Harry, what are you doing?" asked Annabelle. She looked over in amusement at Harry. He was straddled over the hat with his legs on one side and arms propping him up on the other. His face was close up to the hat. "I wanted to see if there were any

22

hairs in the hat," he answered, "but I didn't want to get my trousers wet by kneeling on the grass because Mum would get cross."

"Why are you looking for hairs?" said Annabelle.

"It might be a clue to who took Milly," said Harry excitedly. Both children smiled at each other and a sparkle of hope returned to their eyes.

"Kids! Time to go to school!" shouted Mum.

"Let's meet up at break at the secret place," whispered Annabelle to Harry in the car. He nodded and smiled.

✳ ✳ ✳

As soon as they heard the bell ring for morning break Annabelle and her friend Issy tidied away their books and ran out as fast as they could to the secret meeting place.

Issy was Annabelle's best friend and lived a few streets away from her and Harry. Issy was tall, with brown hair and freckles on her nose. She was in many ways opposite to Annabelle in personality. Where Annabelle was quiet and thoughtful Issy was loud and outspoken. But they shared a love of reading books, always had something exciting to talk about and had a similar sense of humour. They had been inseparable since the day Issy joined the school in Year 1.

The girls ran as fast as they could to the far end of the playground where there was a beautiful cherry tree. At this time of year the soft pink blossom was just starting to bloom. On warm spring days when there was the smell of freshly cut grass in the air the two girls loved to collect the petals that had fallen to the ground. They would pretend to make sweet-smelling perfume with it.

"Do you remember Harry's first day at school?" panted Issy as she ran. "Do you remember that's when you first decided the tree was going to be our secret place?"

"Sssh!" said Annabelle. She tried to turn her head as she ran to see if anyone was watching and almost tripped "We don't want everyone to know about it. I do remember that day really well. It's our safe place. It's a very special tree."

"You told Harry to come here if he needed you or needed to talk about something important? But he never came."

"Not until now," panted Annabelle. The girls looked ahead towards the tree.

"I don't believe it!" exclaimed Annabelle. "Harry and Peter are there before us!"

"They can't be," said Issy. "We got out early from class and have run as fast as we can."

The girls couldn't believe their eyes. Sure enough, there was Harry with his friend Peter. They were busy playing who could knock the other one over. Peter lived on a street near the shop which was on the other side of the church from Annabelle and Harry's house.

Harry and Peter were best friends most of the time. They had known each other since nursery. Peter had a cheeky face, with brown hair and large brown eyes. He was athletic like Harry and loved to run as fast as he could and would climb anything. The two boys were always in competition in whatever they did, which was preferably outside and dangerous.

Annabelle noticed Harry already had mud on his jumper where Peter had successfully knocked him to the floor. "Oh Harry!" she thought.

"We've been waiting for ages," the boys moaned.

"We got here as soon as we could," said Annabelle.

"Peter had his dog Poppy stolen on Monday," said Harry.

"Issy's dog Scally was stolen two weeks ago," said Annabelle. There was a moment's pause as the children all thought about their lost dogs.

"We need to do something with the things we found in the garden," said Annabelle, "I think they might help us find out who took Milly."

"Wow!" said Issy, her big, brown eyes widening. "We didn't find anything when Scally was stolen. She just disappeared. One minute she was there. The next she was gone."

"Same with Poppy," said Peter. "Although to be honest we didn't really look for clues."

"So what things did you find in your garden?" asked Issy.

"We found a large footprint in the soil by the fence. I think it's so big it must be from a man," said Annabelle.

"How do you know it wasn't there before? Could it be your dad's footprint?" asked Issy.

"Dad never helps in the garden!" said Harry, "so it can't be his footprint."

"There was a cigarette end next to the footprint too," added Annabelle. "And nobody we know smokes."

"What else did you find?" asked Peter.

"There was a leather glove and a blue baseball cap lying on the grass. The hat had hairs inside it. I found them. It's the best clue that has been found yet," said Harry proudly, standing tall and puffing his chest out like a peacock. He looked cross when Annabelle took over.

"We found black curly hairs just like Milly's fur on the fence and..." she stopped as she remembered

26

about the blood they had found. The image of the blood flashed into her mind, vivid as a photograph. She paused. Uncharacteristically, Harry had noticed the change in her and held her hand to reassure her. She looked back at the others. "There was blood on the fence."

They all looked down sensing the mood had changed and were unsure what to say next. Issy was the first to speak.

"So you think the footprint was from the person who stole Milly and you think it must be from a man?"

"In that case do you know any men with big feet that could've stolen Milly?" said Peter.

"Well lots of people know we have a dog," said Annabelle. Her mind was racing for the names of possible suspects.

"The blood, hair and footprint were near our neighbour Mr Baker's fence," said Harry. "But he's so lovely. I'm sure he wouldn't dream of hurting any dog. He seems like a real animal lover."

"Okay, well who then?" said Peter.

"What about our other neighbours across the road?" suggested Harry. "Some of them don't like dogs and some of them are a bit odd. Or maybe it was the newspaper delivery man?"

"Our neighbours all know we have a dog and the

man who delivers the papers hates Milly because she barks at him," said Annabelle, writing the names of all the suspects down on a piece of paper.

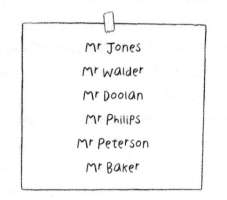

Mr Jones
Mr Walder
Mr Doolan
Mr Philips
Mr Peterson
Mr Baker

"But how can we prove it's any of them? It's hopeless." She placed her hands to her face in despair.

Harry's eyes lit up. "Oh no, it isn't!" he shouted and ran around under the cherry tree, kicking his heels in the air. Peter and Issy laughed heartily at the hilarious little figure who looked like a pixie who has just found a pot of gold.

"Go on then, oh clever one, how do we solve the mystery?" said Annabelle. She felt frustrated that Harry had come up with idea rather than her. But she also felt a rush of excitement that there could be a solution. From the glee on Harry's face it must be a good one too!

"Don't you remember when we compared strands of hair in Mum's science workshop?" he said. "We had to be like real forensic scientists to solve the crime?"

"We compared hairs at the crime scene with the suspects to see who stole the sweets!" exclaimed Annabelle, as she realised what Harry was trying to say.

"Exactly!" said Harry.

"That's brilliant, Harry," said Annabelle. Harry was clearly delighted with himself. "If the neighbours also had a pair of large muddy boots that would be even more evidence. So all we have so far is the hair from the hat. We need to somehow collect samples of hair from our suspects and compare them using Mum's microscope."

"And if you get a match and they also have a big pair of muddy boots you will know who stole Milly," said Issy with smile on her face.

"I could get Mum's microscope and hide it in my room," said Harry.

"You would be good at that," Annabelle laughed.

Harry was a wizard at sneaking sweets, drinks and fruit into his room without their parents' knowledge and never getting caught. That was unless he forgot to eat them and Mum found mouldy apples in his room. The other day she had found five mouldy apples in Harry's room under his bed. She was not impressed and Harry had been banned from the iPad for three days. Although Annabelle was appalled that Harry could do something so naughty, she did admire the fact that he usually seemed to get away with it. She would never have even thought of doing something like that.

"There's a problem," said Issy. "How are you going to collect hairs from the suspects?"

"We could ask Mum to take us round to all the neighbours' houses after school," suggested Annabelle. "We could explain what happened to Milly and ask if they have seen her. All the houses have a porch and everyone keeps their hats, coats and shoes in there. When they open the door, Harry, you could create some kind of distraction. You could fall over or something. That shouldn't be too hard for you! I could then collect hairs from any hats in the porch and look to see if there are any men's boots."

"That's a great plan," said Peter.

The sound of the bell signalled the end of break. The children walked back to their classrooms together. Annabelle pulled Harry aside just before they got back. She looked him in the eye.

"I know we always argue about Milly," said Annabelle.

"But I really do think if we're going to get her back we're going to have to work together. We need to be a team, Harry."

"I agree," he said. "I think we make a great team. I know we'll find who took her, Annabelle! I just know we will!"

Annabelle smiled at him and felt a flutter of excitement in her tummy. The plan was a good one. With her and Harry working together it would not be long until Milly would be safely home again.

Chapter 3

The investigation begins

Annabelle laughed to herself at how easily she and Harry had been able to persuade Mum to take them round to their neighbours' houses.

"I think it's a great idea!" she had said. Annabelle noticed that the look of worry on her face had lifted. So here they all were walking up the flower-filled path towards the house of Mr and Mrs Jones, the elderly couple who lived opposite. Annabelle loved the yellow primroses and daffodils that lined their way.

"Can I ring the bell?" shouted Harry, pushing ahead of them.

"Okay Harry, that's enough. You can stop ringing the bell now," said Mum, pulling Harry's hand away. It took a while but eventually Mrs Jones opened the door. She had a kind face and white grey hair pulled back in a bun.

As the door opened Harry noticed Annabelle step forward so she could see into the porch. Her eyes were like a hawk looking for prey. Harry realised that she was looking for boots and copied her. They both spotted the big pair of green muddy boots at the same time.

"Hello children," said Mrs Jones. "How can I help you?"

"Milly has gone missing," said Mum.

"We wondered if you had seen anything?"

"Why don't you come in?" Mrs Jones beckoned them inside.

"Did you see the boots?" Harry whispered in Annabelle's ear as she squeezed past him. She nodded. Harry then pretended to take a long time taking off his shoes as the others went into the lounge. The wait was excruciating but when Harry finally appeared he grinned at Annabelle.

"I got some hairs from a green cap in the porch," said Harry quietly. "It must belong to Mr Jones. The cap was high up and I couldn't reach it. I had to knock it off with the walking stick!"

"No way! Good work!" said Annabelle, impressed with Harry's quick thinking. Harry was quick to spot the cake Mrs Jones had left on a plate for them all. It was chocolate, his favourite.

"Help yourself, dear," said Mrs Jones, smiling at Harry. It didn't take Harry long to finish the cake. He was busy licking all his fingers when Mum turned to Mrs Jones and explained it was time for them to go.

"Thank you for your help and the lovely cake," she said.

"I hope you find Milly soon," said Mrs Jones waving to them as they walked back down the path.

"Where next?" said Mum.

"Can we go to Mr Walder's house?" asked Annabelle.

"The man who delivers the newspapers?" said Mum. "Are you sure? He's very grumpy and he doesn't really like Milly."

"He might have seen something. Please Mum! He might have some information."

"I've got butterflies in my tummy," said Harry to Annabelle, "What if he's really scary?"

"We have to do this Harry," said Annabelle. "Be brave."

Mr Walder's pathway was overgrown with weeds. The curtains in the lounge were shut and paint peeled from the door. The bell didn't work.

"We're going to have to bang on the door," said Annabelle. Just then there was the sound of heavy footsteps getting louder and the door opened. Mr Walder appeared looking extremely cross. He was unshaven, with dark piercing eyes and his mouth was permanently turned downward. He was a large, intimidating man and looked very angry at being disturbed.

"What do you want?" he shouted.

"The children have lost their dog, Milly, and wondered if you might have seen her?" said Mum. She looked a little frightened as Mr Walder towered over her. It was then that Harry produced a small, multi-coloured bouncy ball. The very same ball he had been asked to put in the bin in case Milly choked on it. He threw the ball into the porch. They all watched as it bounced against the walls then into the lounge.

"Bullseye!" whispered Harry to Annabelle with a look of glee on his face.

"Don't worry Mr Walder. I'll go and get it," said Harry, pushing straight past him and into the house. Annabelle was amazed by his courage.

Mr Walder spluttered, taken aback by the cheek of the young boy. He retreated into the house to retrieve Harry and the ball. Annabelle watched her mum follow them inside. "I'm so sorry," she heard her say to Mr Walder.

Annabelle sprang into action. She didn't have long. A scan of the dirty, dark porch revealed a pair of black muddy boots. The porch was a mess of shoes, coats and hats. Quickly, Annabelle pulled out a plastic bag. She used a pair of tweezers she had taken from her mum's forensic workshop kit to take some hairs from the nearest hat she could find. She was just in time as Mr Walder marched back through the house holding Harry by the arm.

"Now get out of my house and don't come back," he shouted.

"How dare you," said Mum angrily. "Let go of my son." The door slammed in their faces. "Well. What a horrible man," she said. "Are you alright, Harry?"

"Never better! Don't worry Mum. Let's go to the Doolan's house next."

"I'm not sure," said Mum as they made a hasty retreat down the path. "Maybe we should go home."

"Please!" said Annabelle, trying to seem calm despite her heart pumping so hard that she thought it might burst.

Annabelle and Harry put on their most pleading eyes. Mum could not resist. "Okay you two, okay. Stop looking at me like that," she laughed.

They proceeded to visit all the houses on Annabelle's list, until there was only Mr Baker left. So far, only Mr Jones and Mr Walder had muddy boots.

"Thank goodness, we know Mr Baker won't be like Mr Walder," said Mum as they crunched up the gravel path that led to his house. He spotted them from the window and opened the door as they arrived.

"Hello, hello. What brings you here?" he chattered.

"Milly has gone missing. Have you seen her?" asked Annabelle. She felt so relieved. He seemed so happy in comparison to Mr Walder.

"The last time I saw her was yesterday when I spoke to you. You told me how old she was and that she likes eating tomatoes. Sorry to hear she's missing." Annabelle thought he seemed to be genuinely concerned.

Harry and Annabelle watched as Mr Baker and their mum continued chatting.

"You need to distract them Harry," said Annabelle. Immediately Harry ran and fell dramatically onto the gravel. His cry was very convincing. Annabelle was worried for a moment that he had actually hurt himself, but then he caught her eye and stuck up his thumb.

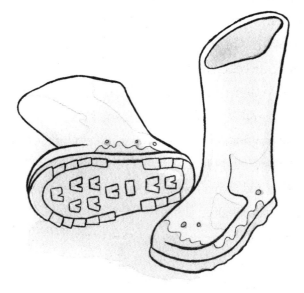

Annabelle watched Mum and Mr Baker run to Harry's side. While no one was looking she ran into the porch. She noted that there was a large pair of black muddy boots sitting on some newspaper just inside the door. There was a mirror in the porch with a shelf below it. She spotted the comb filled with hairs immediately. As quickly as she could she used the tweezers to collect the hairs from the comb. She put them into a bag and put the bag in a different pocket to Mr Walder's sample. She tied a knot in it so she wouldn't mix them up.

She ran outside where Mum had produced a plaster and Mr Baker was helping Harry to stand up. No one had even noticed she was missing. Harry beamed at her.

"Thank you for helping," said Mum to Mr Baker.

"Sorry I couldn't help you find Milly. I'll let you know if I hear anything."

Annabelle felt exhausted. They had been to all their neighbours' houses. But there were only three houses where there had been a pair of large muddy boots.

Annabelle and Harry ran upstairs the minute they got home leaving Mum in the kitchen with her cup of tea.

"Harry, where did you put the microscope?" said Annabelle picking up a piece of paper. He ran to his room and came back shortly with the microscope in his hands.

"I hid it in my toy box," he said proudly. "It's so messy I knew Mum wouldn't look for it in there."

"We have three suspects. Mr Jones, Mr Walder and Mr Baker," said Annabelle. She wrote their names onto the paper and made a column with "BOOTS?" written at the top. She then put a tick next to each of the names. In the next column Annabelle wrote "HAIR COLOUR".

NAME	BOOTS?	HAIR COLOUR
Mr Jones	X	
Mr Walder	X	
Mr Doolan		
Mr Philips		
Mr Peterson		
Mr Baker	X	

"Okay Harry,' she said, "can you get the hair sample from the hat?"

Harry produced a bag with the hairs he had collected from the hat they had found in the garden. Annabelle wrote "hat – suspect" on the bag and carefully picked out several of the hairs using the tweezers. She placed them onto a slide and then, using a syringe, squirted several drops of water on top. She slowly lowered the thin, glass coverslip on top just like Mum had shown them at the forensic workshop.

"It's ready to put under the microscope now," she said. "What colour is the hair, Harry?"

Harry looked down the microscope. The hair came into focus.

"Black and long," he said.

"Have you got Mr Jones's hair?"

Harry produced the bag from his coat pocket and wrote "Mr Jones" on the bag. Annabelle made a slide for Mr Jones's hair sample and wrote his name on it. Harry placed it under the microscope.

"It's grey!" exclaimed Harry. "So it can't be him." Next to Mr Jones's name Annabelle wrote "grey" for hair colour. She then got out the bags with Mr Walder's and Mr Baker's hair samples, and wrote their names on the bags.

"How do you know which is which?" asked Harry.

"I tied a knot in Mr Baker's," she replied and quickly prepared the slides for both men.

"I knew it wasn't Mr Baker," said Harry. "He's got dark brown hair."

"What about Mr Walder? He's so horrible. I bet he did it."

"It's black! It matches the hair from the hat!" shouted out Harry excitedly "Oh! Hold on a minute. These ones are short, and when you compare them they have a different texture!"

"It can't be him either then!" said Annabelle disappointedly, writing down the results.

"Let's face it Harry. This hasn't got us anywhere. It could be anyone."

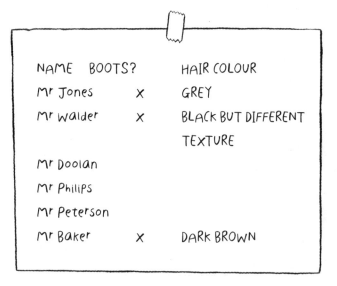

NAME	BOOTS?	HAIR COLOUR
Mr Jones	X	GREY
Mr Walder	X	BLACK BUT DIFFERENT TEXTURE
Mr Doolan		
Mr Philips		
Mr Peterson		
Mr Baker	X	DARK BROWN

"I don't believe it, Annabelle. I really thought it was Mr Walder."

"I know," said Annabelle sadly. "I feel gutted too."

Disheartened, the children hid their equipment and went outside. They were both silent and unsure what to do next, when they heard it.

"Annabelle, did you hear that noise? I thought I heard... but it can't be..."

"I heard it too Harry. It was a whimper. Quiet but definitely a whimper... and it's coming from Mr Baker's garden!"

Chapter 4

Has Milly been found?

Annabelle followed Harry as he quickly climbed up onto the roof of their playhouse. From here they could look over the fence into Mr Baker's garden. She was so excited. It looked like all was lost when the hairs didn't match but she was so sure that she had heard Milly.

"I can't hear the whimpering anymore," said Harry

"Neither can I," said Annabelle joining him on the roof.

"I think it was coming from over there," said Harry pointing at the bottom of Mr Baker's garden.

Both children looked and saw a shed hidden among the apple trees. It had no windows so they couldn't see in and what looked like a big padlock on the door.

"I think Milly is in there," said Annabelle. "I think Mr Baker has taken her and is keeping her in the shed. But it doesn't make sense – the hair didn't match!"

"Quick Annabelle! No time for worrying about the hairs. We need to tell Mum and look in the shed straight away," shouted Harry.

Annabelle followed him as he slid expertly from the roof of the playhouse onto the grass. He ran at breakneck speed into their house. Annabelle followed as fast as she could but she couldn't keep up with her little brother. When she arrived in the kitchen Harry was already pleading with Mum.

"Please Mum! We heard her. We heard Milly. She was whimpering. The noise came from Mr Baker's shed. We've got to go and look now or he'll move her," pleaded Harry. His eyes were wide. Annabelle could see he was anxious as he hopped from foot to foot. Harry now had Mum by the hand and was dragging her to the front door.

"But Mr Baker is so lovely and he loves Milly," said Mum.

"We know what we heard, Mum," said Annabelle convincingly.

"I've never seen you both like this. Okay, just this once we'll go. But I'm sure you must be wrong about Mr Baker."

Annabelle could feel her tummy flipping over as they crunched back up the gravel path towards Mr Baker's house. She felt a mixture of nervousness and excitement. This could be it. In a few minutes she would be able to bury her face in Milly's soft warm fur. She had missed that so much. Once again Mr Baker opened the door as they approached. Annabelle saw a flash of annoyance sweep across his face. Then remembering himself she saw him smile.

"Hello again to you all," he said. "How can I help?"

"I'm so sorry," said Mum. "The children were sure they heard Milly in your garden. They wondered if she'd got stuck in your shed somehow. Would you mind if we had a look?"

Annabelle looked across at Harry. She could see he was as excited as she was. They were only a few minutes away from getting Milly back.

"I'm really sorry," said an apologetic Mr Baker. "I'm just in the middle of an important phone call. I won't be long. Would you mind coming back in ten minutes?"

"Of course!" said Mum. "Sorry to bother you. We'll see you in a few minutes." They returned home where the children waited impatiently in the kitchen.

"This is unbearable," whispered Harry to Annabelle. "We need to get into the shed now!" Harry looked across at Annabelle. Her face was very pale and her beautiful blue eyes were filled with tears. Every second was precious. The tick of the clock in the kitchen became even louder as they waited. Each tick reminding them that vital time was passing. They waited for what seemed like forever in silence.

Finally it was time and they were all crunching back up the gravel pathway to Mr Baker's house. He ushered them into the garden and towards the shed. Annabelle felt her heart beating faster as they got nearer. Her legs were like jelly. Were they too late? She looked across at Harry who was uncharacteristically quiet.

Mr Baker fumbled with the lock on the shed door. It had a combination. He turned his back so the children couldn't see. But Harry crept silently behind him and smiled to himself as he memorised the code unnoticed! Mr Baker threw open the door.

"Here you go children. No Milly in here. I'm really sorry. I know you thought you'd found her. I hope you're not too disappointed," Mr Baker looked at them both with a look of satisfaction.

Harry was the first in. The shed was quite dark inside and smelt musty. There were strange shapes which looked like boxes on either side of the shed. They were covered with blankets. The floor was dirty and cobwebs hung from the ceiling. There was no sign of Milly.

Harry turned to Annabelle "She's not here!" His eyes were cast to the floor. Annabelle checked just to reassure herself that Milly was definitely not there. She took Harry's hand as they walked silently back to their own house. She felt like Mr Baker was laughing at them and could feel his eyes watching them.

"I'm very sorry for disturbing you Mr Baker," said Mum. "Children – say sorry to Mr Baker. I feel really embarrassed. You've been so kind letting us look in your shed."

"No problem at all," said Mr Baker. "If I see anything I'll let you know."

"I know he has Milly!" whispered Harry to Annabelle.

"I agree," said Annabelle. "He had muddy boots in his porch and he looked cross when we asked to look in his shed. He tried to be really nice but I saw his face when he first saw us – he was cross. I think he's putting on an act."

"Do you remember Milly growled at him?" said Harry. "She wouldn't normally do that and we definitely heard whimpering coming from the shed. But what about the hair?"

"I don't understand why the hairs didn't match. It's a mystery. I think we should tell Mum it's him anyway. I really am sure it's him who has taken Milly," said Annabelle.

"She won't believe us. She thinks Mr Baker is really nice. We need more evidence. We need to prove that Mr Baker has taken Milly," said Harry.

"How can we do that? It's impossible," said Annabelle looking desperately at Harry.

Chapter 5
How to Catch a thief

Annabelle looked out of the window of her bedroom and into the garden. It was then that it happened, like a light being switched on, and she realised the answer had been staring her in the face. Her eyes had focused on Mum's laboratory in the garden. She spun round.

"Harry, I've got it!" exclaimed Annabelle. "I know how we can get the evidence to prove it was Mr Baker who stole Milly. We can use DNA!"

Harry looked up from his new Star Wars Lego.

"I don't even know what DNA is!" said Harry, looking unconvinced.

"Yes you do," Annabelle insisted. "Don't you remember Mum told us about it in her 'DNA Detectives' workshop? Okay, how do you know how to make that Lego model of the Droid escape pod?"

Harry picked up the box. "I remember Mum showing us this. I would use the instructions. You're now going to tell me that DNA contains the instructions to make a human."

"What things are in the instructions to make a human, Harry?" asked Annabelle.

"You sound like Mum!" said Harry. "But I know lots of things. I know that DNA contains the instructions to make your heart, eyes, legs, hair colour and your bottom!" Harry laughed at his joke.

"Very funny!" said Annabelle rolling her eyes. She was trying to be serious. "DNA contains the instructions to make everything in your body. All living things have DNA. For example, all plants and animals have DNA. Their DNA contains the instructions to make them. The brilliant thing is everyone and everything's DNA is different."

"Unless you're an identical twin and then your DNA will be the same," said Harry. He was very pleased that he could remember some things from Mum's workshop.

"Don't you remember our favourite bit of the workshop, Harry?" asked Annabelle. "When we got to dress up in overalls, with face masks and gloves – just like real scene-of-crime officers in the police – and collected evidence from a pretend crime scene?"

"I remember," said Harry. "There was a jar of sweets and someone had stolen them. Actually I did steal a few of them when Mum wasn't looking!"

"You're so naughty. Remember Mum told us that

'every contact leaves a trace', so everything we touch will leave a trace of DNA? Look Harry, I'm touching your Lego now and leaving my DNA all over it!"

"Get off!" said Harry, pushing Annabelle away. "I spent ages making that."

"Remember, DNA is all over our bodies," said Annabelle. "DNA is in our skin so, when we touch or rub anything, tiny bits of our skin come off. It's in our blood, our hair roots and our saliva."

"Mum said it's in our snot, our wee and our poo too!" said Harry, gleefully. "Remember at the crime scene in the workshop? We collected hairs, a plaster, snotty tissue and a glass that the suspect had been drinking from and we got DNA from them."

"Do you remember Mum pretended to take DNA samples from all the children at the workshop?" said Annabelle. "We were all suspects. We pretended to send the DNA from the evidence and the suspects to a laboratory and then compared the results."

"Do you remember what the results looked like?" said Harry. "Mum called it a DNA profile. It was a piece of paper with lots of different coloured peaks on it. They had different numbers on them and everyone's was different. I kept mine. It's in my bedroom."

"Do you remember we compared the results from the suspects and the evidence from the crime scene?" said Annabelle. "When we found a match we could work out who stole the sweets. Because the DNA was the same."

"That was brilliant fun," laughed Harry. "Remember it was Peter who'd done it!"

"But don't you see, Harry?" said Annabelle, with excitement. "If we can find some of Milly's fur in the shed we can use it to get DNA. We can then show she was in the shed. Mr Baker must have kept her in a cage or something like that. If his DNA is on the cage and on the things we found in our garden, we can prove he stole her. We'll just need to get a sample from him to compare it with." Annabelle's mind was racing.

"Brilliant Annabelle, but there is one problem. We don't have a laboratory." Harry stopped. His eyes met Annabelle's. "But we do, don't we? Of course! Mum has a laboratory in the garden and she's got all the stuff to get DNA from animals and humans!"

It had taken Harry a while to catch up but he was finally there. This really was so exciting. They were going to carry out a real life version of Mum's "DNA Detectives" workshop to solve a crime. They were going to use DNA to prove who stole Milly.

Annabelle spun Harry around in delight until they got dizzy and fell over. "Harry, we're going to be the real-life 'DNA Detectives'!" It was then Mum came up the stairs.

"Kids! Time for bed! Pyjamas on."

"Tomorrow Harry," whispered Annabelle. "We'll start collecting evidence first thing tomorrow." As the children looked into the mirror to brush their teeth it was clear a sparkle had returned to their eyes. They wished the night would go quickly so they could get started on their most exciting adventure yet.

Chapter 6

The DNA Detectives investigate the scene of the crime

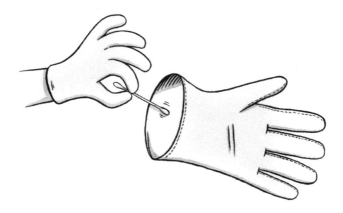

It was early on Saturday morning. Harry came bursting into Annabelle's room sending her door flying. It hit the wall with a crash.

"Sssh!" she said. "Come here quickly, Harry. I've made a list of all the things we need."

"Ready for action, fellow DNA Detective!" said Harry, standing to attention and saluting with a big grin on his face.

Annabelle smiled at her brother. He was such a funny character. He did look like a real soldier on an important mission.

"Okay Harry, these are the things I need you to get. Can you get cotton buds from the bathroom? We can use sandwich bags as evidence bags like we did for the hairs. I'll get them from the kitchen. I'll get the tweezers, overalls, facemasks and gloves from Mum's workshop kit. Can you get a pen to label the evidence? Then meet me at the craft cupboard."

"On it!" said Harry and ran off on his mission.

Annabelle collected the items she needed and then ran quickly to the craft cupboard in the dining room. Of course Harry was there already. How did he do that?

"What do we need from here?" said Harry. Annabelle spoke as she moved aside the paints, glitter and paper to find what she was looking for.

"Plaster of Paris, card, scissors and Sellotape. Why does the Sellotape always disappear? Help me find it, Harry!" Eventually they had what they needed.

"Okay Harry," said Annabelle. "We just need a bottle of water, a spoon and one of those old ice cream tubs from the cupboard in the kitchen."

"I don't get what all this is for, Annabelle."

"We are going to make a mould of the footprint so we can compare it to the boots in Mr Baker's house.

Don't you remember Mum showed us how to do those deer prints we found in the wood?"

"How cool is that? I'm so excited!" said Harry jumping up and down.

Annabelle looked at the kit. It was so professional. She imagined the real scene-of-crime officers arriving in a van with their equipment. She and Harry had hidden it all in their swimming bags. Now to check that the coast was clear. Dad had already gone out to the football and wouldn't be back till later. Mum was cleaning the lounge. The sound of the vacuum cleaner was reassuring. Time to get busy!

"Quick Harry! I think we have about forty minutes before Mum comes into the kitchen for her cup of tea. We have to put on our overalls, facemask and gloves."

"Why though?" asked Harry. "I don't like the facemask. It tickles my nose!"

"Because we don't want to contaminate the evidence with our DNA," said Annabelle. "Don't you remember Mum telling us that?"

She watched Harry struggling into his overalls. "Just think of the overalls like a onesie, Harry. Sit on the floor and then put your feet in!" She laughed as Harry overbalanced and fell face first onto the floor.

"Don't laugh at me!" said Harry, looking very cross. "I'm doing my best!"

They opened the door into the garden. The hat was still lying on the grass, although Harry had removed the hairs which were safely hidden in Annabelle's room.

"We need to get DNA from the hat, Harry. You hold it with the tweezers and I'll swab it with the cotton bud."

"I think the DNA will be around the inside of the hat. Where it rubs against the person's head."

"Well done Harry," said Annabelle. "Just like Mum told us. That's where the bits of skin are most likely to be rubbed off and the skin has lots of DNA in it."

Harry watched his sister rub the material backwards and forwards with the cotton bud. They put the cotton bud into a sandwich bag and the hat in another. Harry labelled them "suspect". Annabelle went over to the cigarette next. This time it was Harry's turn to swab around the end of the cigarette.

"This will have lots of DNA on it," said Annabelle.

"Why?" said Harry.

"Because not only will you have DNA from the skin that has rubbed off inside the mouth when the person was smoking it, but there will be lots of DNA in the saliva," answered Annabelle. The cotton bud and the cigarette were put into bags and labelled. Next was the glove.

"Where will the DNA be in the glove?" asked Harry.

"Think where the skin would rub against it, Harry."

"Inside?"

"Yes!" said Annabelle. "Especially on the top inside bit. That's where the glove would really rub against the skin when the person takes the glove on and off and when they're wearing it."

"I get it!" said Harry. He really loved this swabbing bit. He imagined his swabs would have way more DNA than Annabelle's. In fact his would probably be the main evidence that proved Mr Baker was guilty.

Annabelle knew what was next. It was the bit she was dreading. Both children walked silently to the fence. Without saying anything Annabelle took a cotton bud and wiped the area where the blood was. She looked sadly at the white cotton bud which was now tinged with red at the end. Harry held out the bag. He wasn't sure what to write on the bag, so he labelled it "blood?".

Harry used the tweezers to carefully remove the fur from the fence. They both looked at the black, curly fur and thought of Milly. Only a few days earlier she had been running round with them in the garden. They missed her so much. Annabelle labelled the bag "Milly?".

"Now for the fun bit!" said Annabelle. She cut two long, thick strips of card and checked they would be big enough to fit around the footprint.

She Sellotaped them together and then pushed the card into the soil around the footprint so a large part of the card was sticking out of the soil.

"Harry, empty the plaster of Paris into the ice-cream tub. We are going to need a lot. The footprint is big. Okay, I'll add the water then we need to stir it quickly," Annabelle admired how smooth she had made the plaster. She tipped it onto the footprint.

"Annabelle!" said Harry crossly, "I wanted to do that bit."

"Sorry, I was worried it would set. We need to leave it for thirty minutes. Let's hide the bags with the evidence in that drawer inside the playhouse. No one will look for it there."

"Done it!" said Harry. "Now what?"

"We need a plan. We need to get evidence from Mr Baker's shed. The first thing is how we're going to get into it. We don't know the code for the lock."

"Well I do! I was watching yesterday. It's really easy too – just 1, 1, 1, 1," said Harry proudly.

"You're a star, my man!" said Annabelle. They really were working together as a team to solve this. She felt really proud of her little brother even if he did drive her mad at times "We'll need to go when it's dark so we aren't seen," she said.

"When I think it's safe I'll knock on your bedroom wall tonight Annabelle. Then we can sneak out of the house, climb onto the playhouse roof and over into Mr Baker's garden," said Harry.

"Great! We should leave the kit here so it's ready for us," said Annabelle.

"Do you think the plaster will be ready yet?" said Harry, impatiently.

"I'll have a look." Annabelle gently tapped the plaster. It was solid. She carefully removed the card and turned the plaster over. There was a perfect pattern of the boot imprinted into the plaster. They could see a number of imperfections where the sole of the boot had been damaged and worn.

"If we can find whose boots match this print we'll know who was in our garden and who took Milly," said Annabelle. Both children looked at each other. A bolt of excitement shot through each of them and an infectious smile filled their faces. The evidence against Mr Baker was starting to come together. For once they couldn't wait till bedtime when they could get into the shed and get some more!

Chapter 7

Forensic Investigation of the Shed

After Mum and Dad had put them to bed Annabelle waited patiently in the darkness. It seemed to take forever then finally the signal came. She heard a dull tap against the wall. Annabelle tapped back and then sprang out of bed. She felt almost sick with nerves as she pulled on her wellies, overalls, facemask, gloves and coat. Then she pulled her swimming bag onto her back. She had hidden her outfit under her bed earlier and told Harry to do the same. As she stood up Harry came tip-toeing into her room. She had never known her brother to be so quiet. They both tried not to giggle at how funny they looked in their strange outfits.

"Are you ready?" said Harry. Annabelle gave him the thumbs up. She could see he was not nervous at all. In fact he was buzzing with excitement and wide awake.

"Where's my torch?" he said. Annabelle passed him one of the torches she had in her hand.

"Don't use the torch until we're in the shed," Annabelle whispered in Harry's ear. "We don't want to be seen. It's a bright moon tonight so we should be able to see where we're going. Here is your swimming bag. I thought we could use it to store any evidence we find."

"I can hear the television," said Harry. "I don't think Mum and Dad will come upstairs now. Let's go!" He led the way as they carefully crept down the stairs and out into the garden. Annabelle picked up the kit they needed from the playhouse. She heard a thud as Harry landed in Mr Baker's garden. Trust him not to wait and leave it to her to bring everything! She climbed on top of the playhouse roof and put her legs over the fence.

"Come on, slow coach!" whispered Harry, pulling her legs.

"Don't! I might fall. I don't think I can do it."

"Just jump!" said Harry. He looked up at her face and could see how scared she was "It's alright I'll catch you," he reassured her. "We need to do this for Milly. I know you can do it."

Annabelle closed her eyes, held her breath and jumped. She landed softly on the grass and felt Harry's arms around her helping her up. She let out a long breath and felt relieved she had landed safely. She watched Harry running across the lawn to the shed. He had already undone the lock by the time she got there.

"Well done Harry! That didn't take you long."

"Of course not, I'm a 'DNA Detective'. What did you expect?" he said and gave her a wink. Harry opened the door. The musty smell hit them.

"We can turn on our torches now," said Annabelle. Both children gasped as the light showed a very different picture of the shed than when they'd last seen it. The blankets had gone and behind them were at least seven big cages.

"We were right. This is where Mr Baker was keeping Milly!" said Annabelle.

"It looks like it wasn't just Milly. Look there are blankets in the cages. They've all got hairs on them." Harry peered into the cages. "It looks like they're from different animals. I can see white fur here, black fur and look here is some sandy-coloured fur."

"Quick, Harry! Use the tweezers and collect the fur into bags," said Annabelle. "I'm going to use the cotton bud to swab the handles of the cages. Mr Baker must have touched them and that means he'll have left some of his DNA there. Every contact leaves a trace!" Annabelle got out the cotton buds and started rubbing the cage doors. She used a different cotton bud for each cage, then put them in bags and labelled them.

"Where else do you think he'd have touched?" said Annabelle.

"What about the door handle on the inside of the shed?" said Harry.

"Of course! Good thinking." As Annabelle was walking towards the door she kicked something with her foot. It rolled loudly across the floor.

"What was that?" asked Harry looking up.

"Hold on! I'll have a look." Annabelle shone her torch in the direction the object had rolled.

"Noooo!" she sobbed. Harry was worried. He looked to see what Annabelle was looking at.

"It's a syringe, Harry!"

"What's a syringe?" asked Harry.

"You know, like the needle they put into your skin

when you have to have an injection," said Annabelle. "I think Mr Baker has been drugging the dogs to make them sleepy so they don't make any noise."

"That makes sense," agreed Harry. "Otherwise if Milly was locked up in the shed she'd have barked." He watched Annabelle rub the syringe with a cotton bud.

"But where is she now? And what about the other dogs that were in here?" Annabelle stared at Harry. She saw the frightened look in his eyes and the worry as to where their beloved little dog could be now.

Suddenly the silence was shattered by the sound of heavy footsteps running down the garden. They heard a man's voice shouting gruffly outside. The door of the shed was flung open. The children dropped their torches in fright and the lights went out. Annabelle reached out to Harry in the darkness. They stood together awaiting their fate.

Chapter 8

Caught in the Act!

"I knew it would be you two!" shouted Mr Baker. "Always sticking your noses where they're not wanted!" He moved towards them so that his face was right in front of theirs. He looked furious. "Didn't you find your little doggy?" he mocked. "Poor you! Shame! Get out of my shed now!"

Annabelle took hold of Harry's hand. He was shaking all over. Luckily they had managed to hide the evidence they had collected in their swimming bags. In the dark and with their coats on top Mr Baker had not seen their overalls. Annabelle quickly pulled down her face mask and took off her gloves behind her back so Mr Baker wouldn't see. She nudged Harry with her foot so he would do the same. The last thing they wanted was for Mr Baker to find out what they were up to.

"Right, you're coming with me!" said Mr Baker gruffly and pushed the two children towards his house. Annabelle felt tears in her eyes. But she knew she mustn't cry.

"It'll be alright, Harry, don't worry," she said. She could see that Harry's eyes were wide as saucers and he looked worried. He hated being told off and shouted at, which was surprising considering how many naughty things he did. She put a protective arm around his shoulders which seemed to calm him.

Annabelle cried out as Mr Baker grabbed her arm and pulled her along with him. He gripped it so tightly it hurt. He was a strong man. Harry followed behind them. Annabelle felt relieved as she realised they were heading down the gravel path and towards their own home.

Mr Baker banged angrily on their front door. Annabelle watched as he stepped back from the door. He took a deep breath and released the grip on Annabelle's arm. She rubbed it and put her arms round Harry who was unusually quiet.

As soon as the door opened Annabelle took Harry's hand and pulled him inside their house. They both stood behind Mum peering out at Mr Baker. "Just returning your children!" said Mr Baker. "I found them in my shed!" He was smiling as if he had no cares in the world. A complete turnaround from the man who had just marched them angrily to their house.

"I'm so sorry," stammered Mum. She looked shocked and embarrassed.

"Don't worry at all. I think they just wanted to find Milly. I don't have her, I promise you. Anyway, it's late – I must be off."

The children watched as Mr Baker walked down the path and back to his own house. They knew they were in trouble.

"Right, you two. No iPad for a week. Upstairs and into bed NOW and just think about your behaviour. Poor Mr Baker. I can't believe you did that. You saw how nice he was."

"But he isn't. He hurt Annabelle's arm. He's got Milly and the other dogs who have gone missing. He's the pet thief!"

"No more! Or it'll be two weeks without the iPad!"

"Don't be sad, Harry," said Annabelle when they reached the safety of her bedroom. "I know it was frightening but Mr Baker obviously has something to hide. Don't forget we now have the evidence to prove it's him."

"Oh yes!" said Harry. "I'd forgotten that. We can really teach him a lesson!"

"Tomorrow Harry we're going to break into Mum's laboratory and get DNA from the hair and the cotton buds."

"Brilliant! Like when we extracted DNA from kiwi fruit in Mum's workshop."

"Just like that! Although Mum has a special kit for extracting DNA from humans and animals. Do you remember she showed us when we went in her laboratory? We can use her kit."

"I'm so excited, Annabelle. I can't wait till the morning."

"I know, me too. Remember Granny is coming over tomorrow because Mum and Dad are going out. We need to wear her out. Then after lunch she'll have a snooze. That's when we can get into the laboratory."

"I can't wait! Time for the 'DNA Detectives' to meet some real DNA!" laughed Harry.

Chapter 9
In the laboratory

Their plan worked well. By lunch Harry had exhausted Granny by making her push him really high on the swing in the garden, playing as many different games as possible and continually demanding food. Annabelle peeked around the corner and looked into the lounge.

"It has worked, Harry! Granny is fast asleep!"

"Quick, let's go before she wakes up!" said Harry, who was back to himself after the drama of the night before. They ran to the door of the laboratory in the garden. Annabelle stood in front of the keypad which needed a code in order to get inside.

"What are you doing?" said Harry.

"I'm sprinkling this fingerprint powder on the keypad," said Annabelle. "Mum will have left her fingerprints on the keypad when she types in the code. The powder will make the fingerprints black so we should be able to see which of the numbers Mum uses for the code." She used a brush to dust off the excess powder. "Look Mum's fingerprints! They're on the 1, 2, 4 and 7."

"How do we know what order to press them?" said Harry.

"I hadn't thought of that. Hold on. Those numbers are familiar... it's our birthdays, Harry!"

"Oh yes! You're oldest so maybe the '27' is first. Try it." Harry watched as Annabelle typed in "27" and then "14" They heard the whir of the keypad as it unlocked.

"We did it! Go DNA Detectives!" shouted Harry. Annabelle rolled her eyes. Technically it was her that had done it but she kept quiet. She let Harry have his moment. They were in and that was the most important thing. Getting DNA from the evidence they had collected was key in proving that Mr Baker had stolen Milly. She couldn't wait to get started.

Annabelle loved being in the laboratory. It smelt of chemicals. They often helped Mum with the samples. They knew the layout and where everything was kept really well. The first room was where Mum worked on human DNA. People sent her samples and she used their DNA to find out if they were related and to identify long-lost family members. The second room was for animal DNA. Pet owners would send Mum samples of their pet's fur which contained DNA. The DNA from the pets' fur was then stored in a pet database. If a lost pet was found its DNA could be used to search the pet database. If a match was found the lost dog could then be reunited with its owners.

Annabelle loved the whiteness of the laboratory. Everything felt very clean. There was lots of equipment and machines with flashing lights. It felt like they were on a spaceship from the future. They both put on their white lab coats which Mum kept hanging up for them when they helped in the lab. Then they put on gloves and facemasks so they didn't contaminate the samples with their own DNA.

"The first thing we need to do is print out labels for the samples. How many are there, Harry?"

Harry counted the evidence bags from the shed and the garden.

"Let's see," he said. "There are the cotton buds and hairs from the hat. We also have the cigarette and cotton buds we took from the blood on the fence, the glove, the door handle of the shed, the syringe and from the cages in the shed. That's ten samples."

Annabelle went to Mum's computer. She clicked on the bar codes like Mum had shown her and printed out ten labels recording the numbers in her notepad.

"Harry! Get the tubes and a rack to put them in from the cupboard. Remember Mum uses red racks for human samples," she watched her brother put the rack on the bench. She then put a label on each tube. The tubes were small, about the size of her thumb. They were made of clear plastic with lids on the top.

"Okay, let's add the samples to the tubes. I'll write down what sample goes in each tube. We need to cut the end of the cotton buds off into the tube using these scissors. Remember to wipe the scissors after you use them with this." Annabelle handed Harry a squeezy bottle with a pink liquid in it and some paper towels.

"What's that pink stuff?" he asked.

"Mum uses it to wipe down the benches and wipes things with it to make sure they're clean and to get rid of any DNA. We don't want to contaminate our samples."

Harry used tweezers to carefully add the hairs from the hat to the first tube. Then he cut a small section off the smoking end of the cigarette and added that to the next tube. Harry cut the end off the cotton buds for each of the remaining samples. He carefully placed one into each of the empty tubes, just like Mum had shown him with her samples. She had to get DNA from lots of different things like watches, hats, socks... even toothbrushes! Annabelle recorded which sample went into which tube in her notepad.

"All done!" said Harry proudly.

Next Annabelle got the DNA-extraction kit from the fridge. Mum had shown them how to use it when they extracted their own DNA for fun. She opened the first bottle in the kit. It contained a clear liquid. She carefully added it to each of the tubes.

"What's that?" asked Harry.

"Don't you remember? It's called a 'DNA-extraction buffer'," explained Annabelle.

"Is it like the one we used in the workshop to extract DNA from the kiwi fruit? We made it with washing-up liquid, salt and water. What does it do?"

"Do you remember the instructions to make your Lego Droid Escape Pod? When Mum takes them into schools the instructions can get bashed about and damaged. If our instructions, our DNA, got damaged, we might end up with ten heads or five legs. It's why our DNA is protected in a special bag called a cell."

"What does a cell look like?" asked Harry.

"Imagine some bubble wrap," Annabelle explained. "The bubble bits are like little cells. But, instead of air, imagine they're full of jelly. This is called 'cytoplasm' and it protects the DNA from getting damaged."

"I love popping bubble wrap!' laughed Harry

"Imagine there is a spot in the middle of each cell or bubble in the bubble wrap. That's where the DNA is. It's called the 'nucleus'. The plastic around the outside of the bubble is like the bit on the outside of the cell that keeps all the cell contents inside. It's called the 'cell membrane'. We have cells containing DNA all over our bodies inside and out. They're so small we need a microscope to see them."

"That's great Annabelle, but what does that liquid you added do?" asked Harry.

"Remember the plastic bit on the outside of the bubbles in the bubble wrap?"

"The 'cell membrane'? The bit that keeps all the bits of the cell inside?" asked Harry.

"That's the one!" said Annabelle. "Well, the liquid helps to dissolve the cell membrane and the nucleus and then all the bits inside the cell, including the DNA, spills out into the liquid."

"So all the cells have broken up and the DNA has come out and is in that liquid?"

"That's right, Harry. Now we're going to put the tubes in the water bath." She pointed at a rectangular box with a black lid. There was a number lit up in red lights on the front that said "60°C" and a loud whirring sound coming from the machine. "The water is really hot and will heat up the samples," said Annabelle. "That will totally destroy any cell membranes that are left and all the DNA will be released."

"We've totally blasted the cells!" said Harry in delight. Annabelle set the timer for ten minutes. When the time was up she took the tubes out of the water bath.

"Now we need to put the liquid from each sample through a filter."

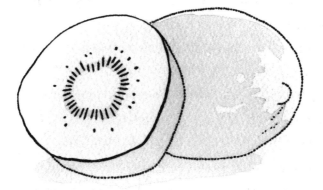

"What's a filter?" Annabelle showed Harry the special tubes with the filter inside which looked like a very small piece of paper. She transferred the liquid from the first set of tubes into the filter.

"A filter is like the sieve Mum puts flour in when she makes cakes to get the lumps out. All the broken up bits of cell get caught in the sieve. The DNA which is dissolved in the liquid goes right through the sieve. Harry watched as a clear liquid slowly dripped out of the bottom of the filter and into another tube. They waited patiently until it had all collected in the bottom of the tube.

"Now to add the alcohol!" said Annabelle. Harry felt his nose tingle as Annabelle added the alcohol. The smell was really strong.

"The salt in the DNA extraction buffer we added at the start makes the DNA clump together and the alcohol makes the DNA come out of solution. If you watch the tube as I tip it gently up and down you will see the DNA appear," explained Annabelle. "There it is! Can you see the white strands?" Harry watched as the two liquids swirled together like ice cubes melting into water. Then suddenly very thin strands like white cotton appeared. It was so exciting. One minute the tube contained only a clear liquid, the next what looked like a ball of white cotton appeared as if by magic!

"How cool is that? Look Annabelle – we have DNA in all our samples. That's amazing!" Both children were delighted. Their eyes sparkled.

"We just have to hook the DNA out with this little plastic hook and put it in this last liquid. This will make sure the DNA is really clean and it can be stored for a long time without being destroyed. If we leave them in the fridge Mum will think they're her samples and will get the results for us. We are finished Harry!" The children quickly cleaned up making sure they left everything as they found it. They ran out of the laboratory and into the lounge to check on Granny. She was still asleep!

"I wish Mum would come home soon so we can get the results. I just hope they've worked," whispered Annabelle to Harry. Both children crossed their fingers.

When Mum and Dad returned later that day Mum proudly announced "I'm going to take the rest of the day off. No lab work till tomorrow!" Annabelle looked at Harry and could see he was as disappointed as her.

"We really need those results" said Harry.

"I know, but hold on a minute," said Annabelle. "Maybe the delay could be just what we need." She suddenly looked very pleased with herself.

"I don't understand," said Harry.

"Well, I just had a thought. If we could get some fur

from Issy and Peter's dogs Scally and Poppy and from Milly we could get DNA from them. If we got DNA from the fur we found in the shed and compared them then we could prove they were in the shed and that it was Milly's fur on the fence!"

"Great idea!" said Harry. The children ran to the kitchen and got a sandwich bag. They then found Milly's brush in the kitchen drawer.

"We need fur with a root on them. You're looking for a little round bit at the end of the hair Harry." They examined the brush carefully and put the hairs into the bag which they labelled "Milly".

"Mum! Can we go round to Issy and Peter's houses to play?" they both pleaded. When Mum wasn't looking Harry winked at Annabelle and she laughed. Mum was completely oblivious to their plan. Annabelle looked at the plastic bag sticking out of Harry's pocket and squeezed the bag in her pocket. Not long now and they would have fur from Scally and Poppy as well as Milly. Then they would break into the lab later and get DNA from the dog's fur.

Soon they would have the proof that Mr Baker had stolen their pets and had kept them hidden in the shed. Her heart pounded with excitement. The results would be ready when they got home from school tomorrow. "Please let the time go quickly," Annabelle whispered to herself.

Chapter 10

The results are in!

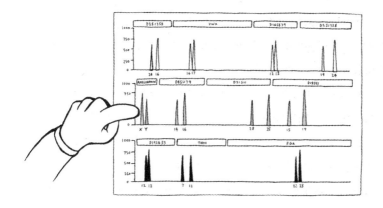

A s soon as they got home from school Annabelle and Harry ran to the kitchen. They looked on the shelf where Mum always left her results ready to post to her clients. Sure enough there were two brown envelopes. Now all they needed was a diversion.

"Watch this!" said Harry, full of glee. He picked up a box of Cheerios and took them into the lounge. Annabelle heard the noise as the entire box was emptied onto the floor followed by a loud cry.

"Mum!" he shouted. Annabelle watched as her mum ran into the lounge and shouted in dismay at Harry. This was her chance. She grabbed her notepad from her book bag and looked up the numbers of their samples. She opened the envelopes, found the correct numbers for the results and took them out. One envelope had the results for the animals, the other for humans. She put the results into her book bag and carefully replaced the envelopes. Quickly she then went into the lounge and helped clear up the rest of the Cheerios which had spilt everywhere!

"Come on, let's go and look at the results," said Annabelle as soon as Mum had left the room. Harry pushed past her, grabbing the book bag from her hand. She laughed as she saw a cascade of Cheerios falling out of his top and trousers as he climbed the stairs. She carefully picked them up as she followed behind him.

"What do the results mean?" he asked as Annabelle entered her bedroom.

"Hold on a minute. You've mixed them all up." Annabelle spread the results out. Using the information in her notepad she sorted them into groups. "Okay, these are the results from the dogs," she said.

"We need to compare these results which have the DNA from the fur we found in the shed with these ones which have the DNA we got from Scally,

Poppy and Milly. If they match then we know they were in Mr Baker's shed," explained Annabelle.

"Like a game of snap," said Harry.

"Exactly!" said Annabelle as she spread out the paper which had the results in front of them. The results from the fur they found in the shed were at the top. The results from the dogs were at the bottom. They both moved forward so they could look closely at the results. On the paper were lots of different coloured peaks and each peak had a different number.

"Snap!" said Harry "Wow! Look these two are the same. Quick look the samples up. Whose sample is it?"

"It's Scally! She was in the shed!" said Annabelle excitedly. "This one matches too... it's... hold on... it's Poppy!" Annabelle dared not look at the last one. She opened one eye and held her breath.

"The last one is a match," announced Harry. He watched Annabelle check the notepad. She beamed.

"It's Milly!" she hugged her little brother and they danced around the room.

"What about the fur on the fence?" asked Harry. Annabelle found the result for that sample.

"It's a match with Milly! So Milly's fur must have got caught on the fence when she was taken from our garden," said Annabelle.

"What about the blood?" Annabelle found the results for the cotton bud taken from the blood they had found on the fence.

"Oh! It didn't work for dog DNA. The paper she held up had no peaks on it. Hold on it worked for human DNA. It's from a human and it's from a man!" exclaimed Annabelle her eyes wide with excitement.

"How do you know that?" said Harry.

"Look at this bit of the pattern here," Annabelle pointed to two green peaks. "Can you see they're labelled 'X' and 'Y'?"

"Yes!" replied Harry staring at the results.

"Well if you're a male, a boy you will have an 'X' and a 'Y' and if you're female, a girl you'll only have an 'X'. It's the 'Y' bit which makes you male. It's the bit of DNA which contains all the instructions to make a male. Girls don't need that bit."

"So we definitely know whoever stole Milly was male and that the blood from the fence wasn't from Milly. What a relief!"

"Let's have a look at the other results," said Annabelle. She spread out the results from the cigarette, hat, glove, syringe, the door handle and the cages. "I expect the results will all match the results from the blood, they will be from the same person."

"You're right! These results match the person

who left their blood on the fence," said Harry. "What are they from?" Harry watched as Annabelle looked at her notepad.

"They're from the cigarette we found in the garden and the syringe. That must have been Mr Baker too."

"But look at these results. There are lots of peaks. Almost double the amount of peaks than in the other results," Harry pointed to another set of results. The children looked and then looked at each other. The results were not as they expected.

"They're from the door handle and the cages. I don't understand. Look Harry – this pattern of peaks from the hat and the glove – it's different from the results for the DNA from the blood."

"But still from a male," said Harry. As he pointed to the X and Y peaks the penny dropped and they both said together: "There are two men!"

"That's why we have so many peaks on the door handle and from the cages. They've both touched these places. So the DNA from both of them is here." The children were delighted to have so many clues! They high fived each other.

"I wonder which of the results is Mr Baker? And who is this second person?" Annabelle put the results next to one another. "There are a lot of

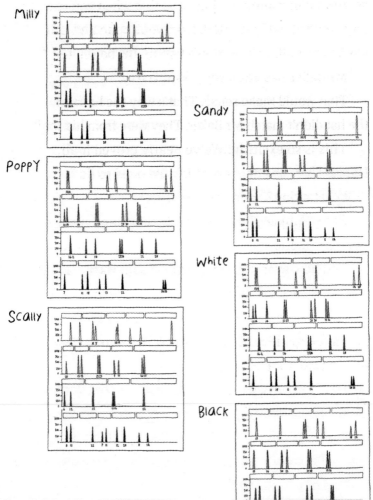

similarities in the patterns from these two," she said. "You see the numbers for the peaks – they share a lot in common. Mum says that when you're a born you get half your DNA from your mum and half from your dad. I think these two might be related."

"Mr Baker has got a son," said Harry.

"That would make sense. That's why the hairs in the hat didn't match Mr Baker. They were from his son!"

"This is so exciting. We've nearly proved it all, Harry. There is one more thing we need to do."

"What's that?" enquired Harry.

"Get a sample of DNA from Mr Baker and his son," said Annabelle

"And how ever will we do that?" said Harry. They looked at each other. It seemed an impossible task. But, to complete the last bit of the jigsaw and prove Mr Baker and his son had taken Milly, surely they had to find a way.

Chapter 11

Collecting the Final Piece of the DNA Jigsaw

The next morning at breakfast Annabelle and Harry excitedly handed an invitation they had made to Mum. Annabelle smiled to herself. She remembered the moment last night when she'd spotted an invite to Issy's birthday party and the idea had come to her. What if they invited Mr Baker and his son to come over for tea and cake after school to say sorry for breaking into his shed? Then they could easily get DNA from both men from anything that they touched and from their coats. Harry had thought it was a great plan. They had made and coloured in the invitation together.

Now Annabelle watched her mum anxiously as she read the invitation trying to guess what her decision would be.

"I think that's a lovely idea, you two. Why don't you go and post it now?" said Mum.

Annabelle felt so relieved. She watched as Harry snatched the invitation from Mum's hand and ran off to Mr Baker's house. He was so quick! Now they would have to wait the whole day to see if the men would agree to come!

The day had passed so slowly but finally here they were waiting by the window to see if Mr Baker and his son would come. Annabelle looked at Harry who was bored. She watched as he squashed his nose against the glass and wiped his face up and down the window.

"That's so gross, Harry. Look at the mess you've left on the glass!"

"Yes, but look how flat I can make my nose," said Harry. "Have a go!" They were so busy they almost didn't see Mr Baker and his son as they walked up the path towards the front door. The knock on the door made them jump.

"So pleased you could come," said Mum showing them into the lounge. "Annabelle and Harry – why don't you get the cakes?"

"Can I take your coats?" said Harry. He winked at Annabelle. She knew he was going to try and get some DNA from the coats like they'd planned. Fingers crossed! Now it was her turn. "Please let this work!" she thought. It really was the very last piece of the jigsaw. If they could get DNA from Mr Baker and his son and match it to the samples from the shed and the garden they could prove the men had taken the dogs.

"Cup of tea for you both?" asked Mum. "Annabelle, why don't you get the chocolate cake?"

Annabelle watched excitedly as the men drank from the cups and used a fork to eat their cake. She remembered what Mum had told them in the forensic workshop: "every contact leaves a trace!" She visualised the cells in their mouths being rubbed off as they ate and drank. All that saliva containing cells being left on the cup and fork. All those cells containing DNA! Please let there be enough.

Meanwhile Harry was very busy. By a stroke of luck Mr Baker had worn the same boots that the children had seen in his house. He had taken them off and left them in their porch when he went inside. They were the boots the children suspected he had been wearing when he stole Milly and had left the footprint in their garden. Harry picked up the left boot and took it into the office which was opposite the lounge. He photocopied the bottom. He was so excited. "I know this boot will match the footprint we found in the garden," he thought. "More proof."

He carefully replaced the boot, put on a pair of gloves and then checked the pockets of the coats. There was no way he would contaminate the evidence with his own DNA! In Mr Baker's coat he found a syringe. He quickly put it into the plastic bag he had hidden in his pocket. Then he used a cotton bud to wipe around the collars and cuffs of both coats. He remembered these were the points where the fabric would rub against the skin, rubbing off all those cells! These bits of the coat would give them the best chance of getting DNA.

Lastly he dug out the Sellotape and pressed the sticky part of the tape onto the coat around the collar. He was delighted. He was able to collect hairs from both coats. He knew he had done well. After hiding the samples upstairs in Annabelle's room he smugly sauntered into the lounge to gloat.

"We're so sorry for breaking into your shed," said Annabelle to Mr Baker. She had her fingers crossed behind her back as she didn't mean it.

"I hope you like your cake," said Harry.

"It's lovely thank you. I think we can forget what happened, don't you?" said Mr Baker.

Annabelle looked at Mum. She looked relieved.

"Have you finished? Can I take out your cups and plates?" said Annabelle so innocently that there was no way the men could know the trap and that the children had planned to collect their DNA!

"How lovely, thank you," said Mr Baker. He was smiling and being so nice. The children could see that Mum had fallen for it but they had not. Mr Baker's son remained quiet. He watched the children closely but they were not phased. How could he possibly guess what they were doing? The children were both looking at his hair. Unlike Mr Baker his hair was long and black. Just like the hairs they had found in the baseball cap they found in the garden! Annabelle gave Harry a knowing look.

Annabelle pulled her jumper over her hands to hide the gloves she had put on and carefully picked up the cups and plates. She didn't want to contaminate them with her own DNA. She was careful to remember not to touch the fork and to remember which person the items had come from.

Once in the kitchen Annabelle used the cotton buds to wipe the cups the men had drunk from and the forks they had used to eat their cake. She carefully labelled the bags and then ran upstairs to hide them in her room. She smiled with delight when she saw the samples Harry had collected. She spotted the photocopy of the footprint. Her tummy flipped over with excitement. It was an Aladdin's cave of evidence! With shaking hands Annabelle pulled out the plaster cast of the footprint they found in the garden. She placed the photocopy next to it. She almost dared not to look. The imperfections where the sole of the boot had been damaged matched perfectly. Mr Baker had been wearing these boots when he had come into their garden to take Milly! She ran as fast as she could downstairs to tell Harry.

"It's a match!" whispered Annabelle when Harry came out into the kitchen. "The boot is a match! Harry, we have so much evidence. We can get into the lab tonight and get the DNA. Mum is in the lab tomorrow processing samples so we should have the results when we get home from school."

"I can't believe you compared the footprints without me. I wanted to do that. I made the photocopy," said Harry, crossly.

"But they match, Harry. Isn't that brilliant? We'll have DNA evidence to prove it was Mr Baker and his son very soon. Did you see Mr Baker's son has long black hair?"

Harry couldn't stay cross for long – this was amazing. Both children were so excited. This was it, the last piece of the jigsaw puzzle. Their hearts raced as they danced with each other around the kitchen. They had collected DNA evidence from right under the very noses of the criminals!

Chapter 12

Can DNA solve the crime and complete the jigsaw?

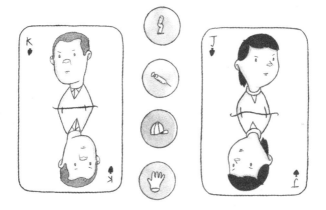

As soon as they were home from school Annabelle and Harry ran into the kitchen to see if the envelope was there. It was! Soon they would have the last piece of the jigsaw in their hands. The excitement was almost too much. "Okay, I'll distract Mum," said Harry. "Watch this!"

"Mum! Where's my Star Wars T-shirt? I need it!" Annabelle heard the sound of footsteps running up the stairs to Harry's room. Quickly she got the notepad out of her book bag and checked the numbers. She then got the results from the envelope. She could see they had worked. Carefully she re-sealed the envelope and put the results into her book bag. Then she went to find Harry.

By the time she got to his room two drawers of clothes had been emptied onto the floor with no sign of the Star Wars T-shirt. Harry was happily tossing clothes into the air and all over the floor while Mum searched through them. When Harry saw Annabelle he reached behind his pillow, pulled out the T-shirt and shouted: "found it, Mum!"

"Harry!" said Mum crossly. "Can you put these clothes away? I'm off for a cup of tea." The children waited till Mum was safely downstairs. They ran to Annabelle's room. Harry grabbed the book bag and spread out the results on the floor.

"Do you remember the DNA from the cigarette we found in the garden and the DNA from the syringe was from one man?" said Harry. "I'm going to put them here. The DNA from the hat and the glove were from a different man. I'm going to put them here. Now we just have to match them up and see who is who." Harry watched as Annabelle placed the results in two different positions on her bed.

The children looked at the samples on the floor. "Harry, help me sort these out," said Annabelle as she checked her notepad. "Samples 21 to 25 are from Mr Baker. They're from the fork, cup, coat and hairs on the coat." Harry carefully placed them all together. They all matched.

"Samples 26 to 30 are from Mr Baker's son," said Annabelle. Harry placed all the samples in a separate pile.

"They all match too, Annabelle. But look – they're different from Mr Baker, as they should be."

"Harry, you take Mr Baker's samples and match them up to the samples on the bed. I'll take Mr Baker's son's samples."

"It's like criminal snap!" laughed Harry.

"Criminal bingo!" laughed Annabelle. Then at the same time they both shouted "snap!"

"It's a match, Harry! The DNA from the baseball cap and glove match with the DNA from Mr Baker's son. They belong to him. He was in our garden!"

"I've a match too!" said Harry. "The DNA from the cigarette we found in the garden match with the DNA from Mr Baker and it's his DNA on the syringes."

"Look Annabelle, you can see DNA from Mr Baker and his son in the samples from the cages and door handles."

"We've done it, Harry! We have the missing link, the proof that both men were in our garden when Milly was stolen. We have the DNA from Scally, Poppy and Milly to show the dogs were in the shed. We can also show that both men were in the shed and touched the cages and door handle and that Mr Baker was using whatever was in the syringes to drug the dogs. It's time to tell Mum."

"What if she doesn't believe us? She's going to be cross that we broke into her lab," said Harry.

"If we don't, then we won't get Milly back. We have to do this, Harry," said Annabelle. Still, she felt sick with worry at what Mum would say. Annabelle hated doing anything wrong and getting in trouble. They'd lied but with a good reason.

As they expected, Mum was furious when she found out that they had broken into her lab, not just once but several times. She was utterly dumbfounded when Annabelle described how they'd collected samples from Mr Baker and his son without their knowledge. Initially she couldn't speak and the three of them sat in an unnerving silence while the children awaited their fate. The evidence they had collected was spread across the kitchen table.

"I don't know what to say. I'm so cross with you both," said Mum. "All the lies and sneaking around.

Going into my lab without my permission and using my things. Worst of all you should never take someone's DNA without their permission. I just don't know how much trouble you might be in. I have to say the evidence you've collected is really strong. But I don't think the police can use it because of the way you've got it. What a mess. I'm so cross with you but I know why you did it. I have to admit: scientifically, what you've achieved is incredible. I don't know what to do!" Mum held her head in her hands. Then suddenly she jumped up.

"Wait here!" she said and disappeared into the lounge.

"I think she's going to call the police," said Harry.

"Quiet! Let's try and hear what she's doing." Harry opened the door and they both listened carefully. They could hear a muffled conversation. It went on for long time. Then there was the sound of footsteps and the door to the kitchen opened. Both children quickly returned to where they had been sitting.

"I've spoken to the police," said Mum. A big grin filled her face. "They're on their way to arrest Mr Baker and his son and search the shed and their house. They want to talk to you both and see your evidence."

"Are we in trouble?" said Harry looking worried.

"No, not with the police, although they want to

make it clear to you both that you must never take someone's DNA without their permission. But you're still in a little bit of trouble with me. Please cheer up you two – you've done it! You solved the mystery and hopefully they'll find the dogs next door and our lovely Milly. It's time to celebrate!" said Mum, holding out her arms for a hug.

Annabelle rushed in for a group hug with Mum and Harry. There was a real warmth and happiness as they all held each other tightly. If Milly was here she'd have joined in too thought Annabelle smiling to herself. She loved it when Milly did that. Milly knew what "group hug" meant! Soon their little dog would be back home and it was all thanks to the "DNA Detectives".

Chapter 13

An anxious wait

The children watched with excitement as two police cars pulled up outside their house. Two police officers got out of the first car. They went to Mr Baker's house and knocked on the door. The door opened. Shortly afterwards the children watched the police officers march Mr Baker and his son to their police car. The first police car then drove away. Next there was a knock on their door. It was the police officers from the second car.

The police wanted to see all the evidence the children had gathered. Annabelle and Harry were proud to show them everything. They carefully explained to the police officers where the evidence had come from and how they had collected it. Annabelle handed over her notepad and the plaster cast of the footprint. Mum showed them the lab and Annabelle and Harry proudly explained how they had got DNA from the samples. They also showed them where they had found the evidence in the garden.

Annabelle could see the policemen were surprised at the amount of evidence they had collected.

"I think you're after our jobs!" said one of the policemen. "You are mini detectives."

"No!" Harry replied. "We're the DNA Detectives!"

The policeman winked at Harry "You certainly are, young man. This is all very impressive. Although I think your Mum has explained that you must never take DNA without someone's permission. Also, the evidence must be collected by our scene-of-crime officers if we want to make sure that the criminals are found guilty and sent to prison. With a bit of luck, though, if what you're saying about your neighbours is true, there may be enough evidence left for us to collect."

Annabelle looked at Harry. His smile matched hers going from ear to ear. The police officers left shortly after but next door the searches of the house and the shed went on all day. The children could hear lots of banging about on the other side of the walls. They watched from Annabelle's bedroom window as scene-of-crime officers went into the shed dressed just like Annabelle and Harry had been, in white overalls with facemasks and gloves.

Much later there was a knock at their front door. It was another policeman. Dad got up and answered the door. "You two stay here," he said smiling at them.

"He's probably come to tell us they've found Milly!" said Annabelle. It was unbearable to have to wait. Harry was fidgeting up and down on the sofa in nervous anticipation. They heard the door shut and watched the policeman walk away down the path.

"I can't hear Milly," said Harry.

"Maybe she's still sleepy from being drugged," said Annabelle. The door opened. The children could tell from their Dad's face it was not good news. They both sat down dreading what he was going to say.

"I'm so sorry. I've bad news. The police have done a thorough search of the house and the shed. They couldn't find anything."

"That can't be true," pleaded the children. "We know they took Milly. We have the proof. What about the cages in the shed?"

"They've gone. The police didn't find any cages. There was nothing in the shed. They couldn't find evidence of any dogs being kept in the shed or anywhere in the house. I'm so sorry, children. They've had to release Mr Baker and his son."

Annabelle felt her Dad's arms around her giving her a hug. She sobbed uncontrollably. Mum had come in and was hugging Harry. He was really cross. "It's not true. It can't be true," he said, over and over again.

"Look why don't you two go downstairs into the cellar and play some table football? I'll bring down some of those chocolate chip cookies you like. We'll find her," said Mum, although Annabelle didn't think she sounded convinced. They had been so close. How could this all be happening?

The children opened the trap door in the middle of the kitchen floor and walked down the stairs into the cellar. In the past the cellar was used by families to store coal. Some of their neighbours used theirs as a wine cellar but luckily for Annabelle and Harry their parents had turned it into a games room. Usually they would spend hours trying to beat each other at table football but today they just sat on the floor with their backs against the wall and their heads in their hands.

"I don't really feel like playing football," said Harry. "I'm not sure I even want a cookie."

Annabelle knew if Harry didn't want to eat he must be feeling really sad. She gave him a hug.

"They must've taken all the cages out and hidden them," said Annabelle "Maybe they knew we were onto them."

They sat in silence for a while when both children heard a whimper. It was muffled but definitely a whimper.

"Did you hear that?" said Harry. "I thought I heard a dog!"

"I did too. It's coming from behind that wall," said Annabelle. She pressed her ear against the wall so she could hear better. Harry copied her as the sound came again. "It's Milly! I'm sure it's Milly," said Annabelle, her voice full of hope. "I think she heard our voices and is letting us know she's there."

"What if Mr Baker is keeping the dogs in his cellar? All the houses along the street have cellars. Maybe the door to Mr Baker's cellar is hidden and that's why the police didn't find it?" said Harry.

"We've got to get into his cellar and look. We need to be quick before they remove any more evidence. Come on, Harry, we need to get a kit together. Can you get a torch, sandwich bags for evidence and cotton buds? I'll get string, a screwdriver, Sellotape and a camera. This time we'll photograph the evidence. They can't argue with that."

"But the police said only their scene-of-crime officers should collect the evidence" said Harry, looking worried.

"There's no time to argue, Harry. We need to get Milly before they move her. I'm sure she's in their cellar."

"Can't we just tell the police we think the dogs are in the cellar and they can go and have a look?"

"They won't believe us Harry. They found no evidence in the shed or the house. They think we made it up. Come on! Go and get the kit and meet me in the lounge. We need to wait for Mr Baker and his son to go out."

Annabelle and Harry pretended to watch television but secretly they were watching to see when their neighbours left the house. The men had returned to the house at least two hours ago after being released by the police. Just when the children thought they would never go out they heard the sound of a car engine. They watched as both men drove off in their car. Annabelle pulled on the backpack which contained their detective kit. "Mum, we are just going round to Issy's house," said Annabelle.

"Okay!" shouted Mum. "Be back for tea, please!"

"See you later!" shouted the children as they rushed out into the garden. They climbed up onto the playhouse roof and then onto the fence where they both jumped straight down into Mr Baker's garden. This time Annabelle didn't stop. She was scared of jumping down from the fence just like last time but she knew they didn't have long to find Milly. There was no time for any delays no matter how scared she was.

"How are we going to get into the cellar?" said Harry.

"We're going to slide down the coal chute!" laughed Annabelle.

"The what?"

"The coal chute! It's a small tunnel, a bit like a slide which leads down into the cellar," explained Annabelle. "People used to tip coal down the chute as it was a quick way of getting the coal into the cellar. You know that little window in the back wall of our house? Well, that's the entrance to our coal chute. Mr Baker must have one in a similar position in his house. Help me look for it, Harry."

"I think it might be under here," said Harry pointing at some planks of wood which were leaning up against the back wall of Mr Baker's house. "Help me move them." The children worked together to move the planks, which were heavy and wet.

"Uurgh! They're covered in slugs and snails," shrieked Annabelle.

"I love snails and slugs!" said Harry in delight.

"Wow! Some of them are huge. This is brilliant!"

"Come on," said Annabel, impatiently. "We haven't got time for that. Look, here it is! That little window is the entrance to the coal chute. Just like it is in our house. Pass me the screwdriver from the bag and I'll see if I can open it." Luckily the little window was very rusty and the damp had made the wooden frame soft. Annabelle was able to lever it open easily. There was enough space for them to squeeze in.

"Harry, can you see if you can pull some of the planks over the entrance so it looks like it hasn't been disturbed? Shall I go first?" Harry peered into the darkness. He wasn't sure if he wanted to slide down there.

"Okay. You go first, Annabelle. Be careful though." Annabelle nervously climbed into the coal chute. It was made of brick and seemed to go down a long way. It was so dark she couldn't see the bottom. The walls felt slimy and smelt of damp. She took a deep breath and slid down into the darkness letting out a shriek as she plummeted downwards. Harry pulled the planks over the entrance behind him and quickly followed her. His heart thumped hard in his chest with fear and excitement.

Chapter 14

A Slide into the unknown

"Ouch!" exclaimed Annabelle as Harry slid down the coal chute and landed right on top of her. It was pitch black in the cellar apart from a few shafts of light coming in from the window at the top of the coal chute. The room felt cold and smelt of damp mixed with bleach and a strong doggy smell.

"We're not going to be able to climb back out," said Harry, looking back up at the coal chute. As their eyes became accustomed to the dark they could see the coal chute came to an abrupt stop half way up the wall. Then there was a long drop to the floor of about two metres where they were now sitting in a heap. Luckily a pile of dusty old blankets had cushioned their fall.

"There's no way we can get back up to the coal chute to climb out. It's too high up and the walls are too slippy to climb out," said Harry.

"Don't worry, we'll find a way. Let's see if we can find Milly. Hold on I'll switch on the torch," said Annabelle. She could see black shapes all around them in the dark but couldn't make out what they were. Annabelle shone the light around the small, damp cellar. The black shapes all around them were suddenly lit up and started to make sense.

"Look Harry – cages!" exclaimed Annabelle. "I think there are animals inside them."

The children ran round shining their torches in the cages. It was then that they found her.

"Harry, quick," said Annabelle excitedly.

"You've got to come quickly... It's Milly!"

Harry ran as fast as he could to where Annabelle was shining her torch so he could see for himself. He looked in and there she was – their beloved little black dog, Milly. With a seemingly huge effort the little dog in the cage lifted her head and was just able to wag her tail. The children stuck their fingers through the bars to try and touch her. They had found her!

"Milly! We missed you. We've been looking for you. Are you okay? Oh Milly," said Harry breathlessly, stroking her nose with his finger. Her beautiful big brown eyes looked adoringly into his eyes.

"She must've been drugged," said Annabelle. "She's really drowsy."

"Her cage is on the wall nearest our cellar. It must've been Milly who we heard when we went to play table football. Bless her! She must have wanted us to know she was here."

They could see there were at least five other cages with dogs in them. But the room was silent.

"None of the dogs are making a sound," noted Annabelle, peering through the darkness. "Look – they're all lying down. They must be drugged."

"I'm sure that one there is Poppy. And, hold on, this one is definitely Scally. Look – there are two, no, hold on, three other dogs." The children quickly counted the dogs. There were six in total. The cages were very small and cramped, each with a padlock on the outside securing the doors. Inside every cage was an old blanket, some newspapers spread on the floor and a dirty bowl with some water in it.

The children could see the water bowls were

secured to the cage with old bits of wire to stop the dogs tipping them over. Scattered on the floor were the discarded syringes the men had been using to drug the dogs. The room also smelt of bleach presumably to clean the cages, and in the corner was a black bag containing the dirty newspaper.

"That bag stinks!" said Harry, holding his nose.

"We need to get Milly out," said Annabelle, anxiously. "Look those steps must lead to the trap door in the kitchen. Just like it does in our house. Let's see if the trap door at the top is open."

They were just climbing the stairs when they heard a noise.

"I can hear voices," whispered Harry.

"Oh no! It's Mr Baker and his son. They're back. We need to hide." The children were terrified that they would be discovered.

"Quick Harry, get under those blankets and lie as flat as you can," said Annabelle, urgently pointing to the pile of blankets which they had dropped onto when they slid into the cellar. She turned off her torch and Harry did the same.

The children concealed themselves under the pile of blankets just in time. They were so scared they almost dared not breathe. The idea of what might happen to them if they were discovered was too frightening to think about. Annabelle reached for Harry's hand. He clasped his big sister's fingers and held them tight. They were alert to every movement in the cellar, their hearts pounding in their chests and the damp and rancid smell of the blankets filled their lungs making them want to cough.

They heard the trap door to the cellar lift open and the sound of footsteps coming down the stairs. A light was switched on.

"Good steal!" said Mr Baker to his son. "Look at this beautiful dog. We'll get lots of money for this one. Hold him still while I inject him."

Annabelle very slowly lifted the blanket just a fraction so both the children could see what was going on. Harry squeezed Annabelle's hand even tighter. The men had a beautiful black Labrador with them. The dog whined when he saw the needle and tried to get away, shaking his head and walking backwards. The children watched in horror as the son picked up a stick from the floor and hit the dog with it.

"Stop messing around!" he shouted aggressively. The dog cowered and then became wobbly on its feet as the drug kicked in.

"Quick! Get him into the cage before he falls over," said Mr Baker. "All these dogs are going tonight. We can't risk keeping them at the house anymore with the police and those troublesome children snooping around. We'll take them to Manchester tonight. Give me that dog's collar. We need to burn the evidence."

The children saw Mr Baker locking the drowsy Labrador into an empty cage. He hung the keys from a nail high up on the wall.

"Are the spare keys there too?" said his son.

"Yep, all there. Quick, check the other dogs and then come on! We need to get the van and get these dogs to Manchester."

"They're all alright. I gave them all a huge dose of drugs so we shouldn't hear anything from them. Let's go."

They heard the men climbing the stairs, push open the trap door, switch off the cellar light and then bang the door shut again before turning a key in the lock. A few seconds later they could hear something being dragged over the trap door. It wasn't long before the front door of the house was slammed closed and they could just make out the noise of a car pulling away outside.

"I think they've gone," said Annabelle. "We don't have long Harry. They're going to collect their van and then they'll take the dogs away. We need to tell the police so they can catch them. We need to get out." She felt like crying but knew she had to be strong.

She dragged Harry from under the blanket and up the stairs, their legs were trembling like jelly. They switched on the light and both pushed up on the trap door to open it. But it was no use. The door was locked.

"It's no good, Annabelle. It's locked. We're trapped. We can't get out. What are we going to do?" Annabelle looked across at Milly. They had to get out of the cellar and tell the police they had found the missing dogs. Otherwise Mr Baker and his son would came back and take the dogs away to Manchester to be sold. Then they would never see Milly again. And what would he do to her and Harry if he found them in the cellar? There must be a way, but how? It was hopeless.

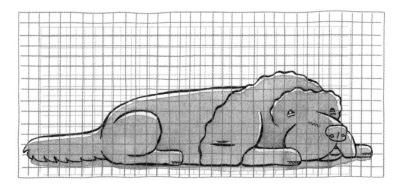

Chapter 15

Trapped!

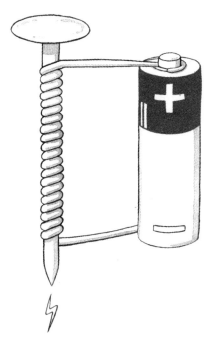

The children stood at the top of the stairs. They looked about, desperately trying to find a way they could escape from the cellar. They were both really frightened and wanted to escape before the men came back. Harry was the first to break the silence.

"I thought I heard Mr Baker ask his son to check if the spare key was in the cellar. Did you hear that?"

"Oh yes, you're right. He did say that. Look up there Harry," Annabelle pointed to the nail on the wall which had the keys for the cages and, what she hoped was, the spare key to the trap door hanging from it. The children took turns trying to jump up and reach the keys with their hands but the keys were too high up and out of their reach.

"What about that stick they hit the dog with. Quick Harry, see if that will reach," said Annabelle. Harry quickly ran over to where the stick had been thrown on the floor. He passed it to Annabelle as she was the tallest.

"It's no good Harry even if I stand on my tip toes I can't reach it."

"What if you pick me up?" said Harry. Annabelle picked Harry up, holding him as high as she could. She staggered about under his weight.

"Be careful! Don't drop me!" said Harry. They were so close but couldn't quite reach to knock the keys off.

"It's no good. They're just out of reach," said Harry sadly. Annabelle carefully put him down. They both sat on the stairs. Harry tapped the torch against his hand.

"Can you stop that please! It's really annoying," said Annabelle feeling scared, anxious and frustrated.

"You're really annoying and I want to go home," said Harry, crossly and nearly in tears.

"Hold on that has given me an idea. We need a magnet," said Annabelle excitedly.

"What gave you that idea? I know, I'll just pop to the shops and get you a magnet, shall I?" said Harry sarcastically.

"You tapping the torch gave me the idea. We're going to make a magnet, Harry. An electromagnet like Mum showed us in her electricity workshop. Don't you remember?" Annabelle smiled.

"Of course! You're a clever big sister. Sorry about before. I'm just scared. I didn't mean it. I just want to get out of here. Tell me what we need and what I can do to help."

"Don't worry, Harry. I feel the same. But you can help. We need a battery which we can take from your torch and a nail. Look – there is one over here by this cage and we need wire. We can use the old wire that has been used to keep the water bowls attached to the cages. We'll also need some string to tie it to the stick. Harry, you get the wire. I'll get the battery, string and the nail." The children sprang into action. They knew that every second counted. By now the men may already be on their way back to the house with the van.

Harry handed Annabelle the wire. The wire was insulated with plastic apart from the ends which were just bare copper strands. Annabelle carefully linked the wire together and then started wrapping it neatly and carefully around the large iron nail she had found on the floor.

"We have to have a complete circuit with no breaks at all or it won't work. The more wire I can wrap around this nail, the stronger the magnet will be. It all has to be wrapped around in the same direction or the current will go in different directions and the magnet won't work."

Annabelle was talking out loud, partly to explain it to Harry but mainly to help herself calm down. Harry watched as Annabelle attached one end of the wire to the battery with Sellotape from the backpack. She then attached the other end of the wire to the opposite end of the black and gold coloured battery.

"Help me attach it to the stick, Harry. We have to do it quickly before the battery runs out. It must be working I can feel it getting hot. See if that other nail on the floor over there sticks to it."

"Yes! Get in. It works!" said Harry in delight as the nail stuck to the wire. Quickly the stick was hoisted in the air. With the homemade electromagnet at the end and Annabelle holding Harry as high as she could they were able to reach up to where the keys were dangling from the nail on the wall. He aimed the magnet at the keys. There was a satisfying click as the keys attached themselves to the magnet. Harry lifted them free from the nail and slowly lowered them down.

"Yes! We did it!" said Annabelle. She put Harry down and shook her arms which ached with holding on to him so tightly. She couldn't believe how heavy her little brother was. It must be all that pizza he ate!

Harry pulled the keys off the magnet and ran as fast he could over to the cage where Milly lay. As he unlocked the padlock and opened the cage door, Harry watched as Milly's tail wagged. With an effort Milly turned her head and tried to lick Harry. It was almost as if she was saying: "thanks for rescuing me".

Annabelle stood behind Harry. "She's still really drowsy," she said "I don't think she'll be able to walk. I'll carry her. We must shut the cage door too so it doesn't look like anyone has been here."

"Harry, grab the backpack and the stick then go and unlock the trap door. I feel really bad we can't get the other dogs but if we do the men will know we've been here. Hopefully they won't spot that Milly is missing. Once we get home we can send the police in for the other dogs. Come on! We need to get out of here right now!"

Annabelle gathered Milly up in her arms. She felt the little dog snuggle into her as she followed Harry and ran up the stairs. Her heart was beating like an express train. She watched as Harry turned the key in the lock. Would it open? The children almost couldn't look both fearing that the key wouldn't work. But then with a single turn came the satisfying sound of the lock clicking open. Harry tried to push the trap door. But it wouldn't move.

"There's something on top of it. Help me Annabelle," he said. Laying Milly gently down on the top step Annabelle joined her brother in pushing the door. Slowly it moved. The children kept pushing.

"Did you hear that? That scraping sound," said Harry.

"It must've been whatever was pushed over the trap door. We must be moving it, whatever it is. Keep pushing I think we're nearly there. Please don't let the men come back now," said Annabelle. She felt really frightened. Gradually the trap door was opening. The children gave one last big push then all of a sudden the door gave way and swung open.

"We've done it! Harry, we are free!" the children hugged each other as the light from the kitchen came flooding in. The fresh air was very welcome after the damp doggy smell that filled the cellar. There was no time to celebrate or collect evidence

– they needed to get out of the kitchen and to the safety of their own house.

"We need to cover our tracks so the men don't know we've been here. Quick Harry, turn the light to the cellar off and lock the trap door. I'll get Milly. Look: this table and rug were covering the door. That's why we couldn't get the trap door open and why the police didn't find the cellar." The children both looked at the red woollen rug and wooden kitchen table now dislodged by their actions.

"Come on Annabelle, we need to put everything back where it was. Hopefully the men won't realise that one of the dogs is missing." The children pulled the rug back over the door and dragged the heavy table back into place.

Annabelle carefully picked Milly up from the kitchen floor. "Follow me!" she shouted to her little brother as she ran towards to the front door. She knew the way as it was in the same place as in their house. Harry was close behind. Milly licked Annabelle's face as she opened the door. Normally this would've made Annabelle laugh but she needed to concentrate. A cold wind blew in as the door swung open. The children leapt through it to the freedom of the front garden. They turned and made sure they closed the front door behind them before sprinting as fast as their legs would carry them down the path for home. They looked straight ahead, not daring to look back in case the men returned.

"We're almost there! Keep going," encouraged Annabelle. She had never run so fast in her life. She was running so fast that she had kept up with Harry! The children burst through their front door almost knocking over Mum. They were completely out of breath, dirty from being in the cellar and shaking with nerves and excitement at what had just happened.

"We've got her, Mum! We rescued Milly from next door!" All eyes turned to the familiar little back dog lying in Annabelle's arms. Milly managed to wag her tail three times as she realised she was finally back home with her family where she belonged.

Chapter 16

DNA Detectives catch pet thief!

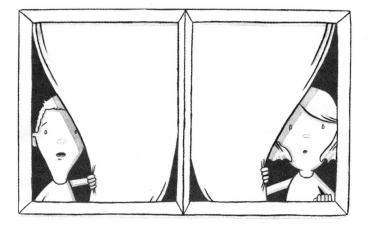

Tnhe children sat in the lounge with Milly snuggled next to them under a blanket on the sofa. Annabelle gently stroked Milly's head which was resting on her lap. She thought how content and happy Milly seemed. In the background they could hear Mum telling the police what had happened.

"I hope she tells them they have to come quickly and that the dogs are in the cellar," said Harry, " or the men could get away."

"I think she will. We did tell her that it was really important and where to find the dogs," said Annabelle. Just then the door opened and in came Mum.

"The police are on their way. We need to stay inside so we don't get in their way and we need to keep out of sight. Why don't you go and play upstairs?" Annabelle and Harry didn't need to be told twice. They ran up to Harry's room which was at the front of the house and took up positions either side of the curtains.

"Mum said we weren't to be seen," said Annabelle, worried she might get caught doing the opposite of what Mum had said.

"Don't be silly," said Harry. "Why would they look up here? Just keep still and we can watch what happens. She only said we weren't to be seen and we won't! Chill out big sister – eyes on the prize!" Harry winked at her, pointed at his eyes and then out of the window towards Mr Baker's house.

"Look – those must be the police officers. They've parked out of sight. Some of them are going into the back garden. Goodness, they had better be quick. I think that's Mr Baker's van!" Annabelle and Harry watched as a large rusty white van pulled into the drive outside Mr Baker's house.

"Look – Mr Baker and his son are going into the house." There was an agonising delay when nothing happened and everything was silent. It was almost unbearable and then it all happened very quickly. The children watched police cars and a van pull up with a screech outside the house. A large number of policemen piled out of the van and stormed into the house from all directions. There was the sound of banging and crashing and then silence once more.

"Look Annabelle: Mr Baker's front door is opening." Sure enough the door opened. Out came Mr Baker and his son being marched in hand cuffs down the path to the waiting police car. Harry stood up to get a better view at which point seeing the curtains move Mr Baker looked up.

"He looks furious! Harry, quick, bob down again." The police car drove off with the two men inside. Next a police dog-handlers van appeared and what looked like an RSPCA officer. It seemed like a long time but the children watched as the remaining dogs were brought out and into the awaiting vans. The policemen had to carry some of the dogs but some were able to walk although they were very wobbly on their feet.

"Look: there's a police officer coming to our house," said Annabelle. They heard a knock on the front door.

"Children, can you come down?" shouted Mum. "There's a police officer here to talk to you." With much excitement the children ran downstairs and spoke to the police officer. He had a big smile on his face. He told the children they had caught the two men red-handed in the cellar with the dogs. When he asked if they had any further information the children didn't know where to start!

"They were going to take the dogs to Manchester to sell," said Annabelle. "They've been drugging them to keep them quiet and if you look on the floor in the cellar you will find all the used syringes. The second man is Mr Baker's son – we proved that using DNA."

"They took off the dogs' collars and burnt them," said Harry. "If you look in the fire you'll find the tags from the collars. It might help you identify the dogs. If not, we have the DNA from our friend's dogs and proof that two of the missing dogs are Poppy and Scally."

"Wow!" said the police officer. "You've been really busy. Thank you for all this information. It'll be really useful. I'm just going to radio over now to tell the scene-of-crime officers to look in the fire and for the syringes. We'll keep you informed of what's happening."

Later the children watched the scene-of-crime officers enter the house in their white overalls. Their thoughts turned with excitement to all the evidence the officers would be busy collecting using their tweezers, evidence bags and cotton buds. Although the officers would call them swabs!

"There's so much evidence in the cellar for the police to find, Harry. All that DNA on the cages, the syringes, the hair from the pets and the stick. There is probably a lot more too."

"Maybe it's a good thing we didn't have time to collect it. We wouldn't have wanted to destroy any evidence that could be used to convict Mr Baker and his son."

Annabelle looked over at Harry with a big smile on her face. As a special treat Mum had said Harry could sleep over in Annabelle's room. Milly was curled up in between them as an extra special treat. She looked delighted to be there. Annabelle thought how tired she was but when she looked over at Harry she laughed to herself. He was nearly asleep already with one arm around Milly and starting to snore! She was in for a noisy night. Maybe this wasn't such a treat. Mum and Dad poked their heads around the door.

"We're so proud of you both. Our very own 'DNA Detectives'! Well done and sleep tight!"

Issy and Peter's parents called in the morning to thank the children for finding Scally and Poppy. Both dogs had been returned to their rightful homes that morning. The police had used the DNA evidence Annabelle and Harry had provided to identify the dogs. The police had also asked if Mum would get

DNA from the remaining dogs that had been found and run the results through her database. She found matches and the remaining three dogs were returned to their delighted families.

Next the phone rang again. This time Dad answered it. When he finished the call his face was beaming. "I've exciting news!" he said. "Mr Baker and his son have been charged with stealing pets which apparently they have been doing for a long time. They have both pleaded guilty and it looks like they'll be off to prison! The police are really impressed with all the help the 'DNA Detectives' have given them to catch this pair. To say thank you they would like to invite you to be their special guests of honour at a display by the police-dog display team at the local show. Oh, and a journalist called earlier. They would like to publish the story in the local paper."

So there it was: the first case for the "DNA Detectives" published in the local paper. Annabelle proudly cut out the story and pinned it up on the wall in her room. She kept reading the headline: "DNA DETECTIVES CATCH PET THIEF!" She loved the photograph of her and Harry sitting in pride of place watching the police dog display team with Milly sitting on her lap. She shivered with excitement as she thought of the amazing adventure they had just been through. Surely this was not the end of the "DNA Detectives"? She smiled as she thought about the forensic kit that she and Harry had hidden under her bed.

"No!" she thought triumphantly. "This was definitely not the end of the 'DNA Detectives'. No, this was just the very start of their adventures!"

D·N·A Detectives catch pet thief!

Acknowledgements

There are so many people I would like to thank
who have helped me with this book but first
and foremost I would like to thank my children,
Annabelle and Harry and our dog Milly who were
the inspiration for the characters in this book.
They have given me so much material and great
memories to write about! I would also like to thank
my husband, Jonathan, who has been instrumental
in getting this book to where it is and been
incredibly supportive throughout. Thank you for
your patience and commitment! I will always be
very grateful for all your help. A big thank you to
my Mum and Dad, Debbie, Ant, Alice, Emily, Alan,
Virginia, Chris, Jo, Evie, Issy, Joanna, Nick, Alex
and Peter for reading the book and giving me your

valuable feedback. I am very grateful for all your enthusiasm and the encouragement you have given me. What a great family!

I would also like to thank Ben Duffy at St James's House Publishing and my book agent Chloe Seager at Diane Banks Associates for believing in me and making my dream become a reality.

A very special thank you to Jamie Maxwell for providing the fantastic illustrations for this book. You really have brought the story to life. Thank you for capturing the spirit of the book and its characters. You are incredibly gifted at what you do.

A huge thank you to the public-engagement team at the Sanger Institute in Cambridge – Ken, Steve, Fran, Emily and Becky – for your encouragement, advice, support and helping with the web links for this book.

Finally thank you to all my friends, all the families who attend my DNA workshops/stories and to the children at the many schools, libraries and home-schooling groups who I have met through my work. Your excitement and encouragement when I have told you about this book has meant so much to me. It is finally here and you get to read it! Thank you for all your support. It is magical sharing my love of science with you all.